MW00593484

Cross-Dressing Villainess Cecilia Sylvie

3

Hiroro Akizakura

Illustration by **Dangmill**

YEN ON

NEW YORK

Cross-Dressing Villainess Cecilia Sylvie 3

Hiroro Akizakura

TRANSLATION BY KIKI PIATKOWSKA ❀ COVER ART BY DANGMILL

This book is a work of fiction. Names, characters, places, and incidents are the product of the author's imagination or are used fictitiously. Any resemblance to actual events, locales, or persons, living or dead, is coincidental.

AKUYAKU REIJO, CECILIA SYLVIE WA SHINITAKUNAI
NODE DANSO SURUKOTO NI SHITA. Vol.3
©Hiroro Akizakura 2021
First published in Japan in 2021 by KADOKAWA CORPORATION, Tokyo.
English translation rights arranged with KADOKAWA CORPORATION, Tokyo,
through TUTTLE-MORI AGENCY, INC., Tokyo.

English translation © 2022 by Yen Press, LLC

Yen Press, LLC supports the right to free expression and the value of copyright. The purpose of copyright is to encourage writers and artists to produce the creative works that enrich our culture.

The scanning, uploading, and distribution of this book without permission is a theft of the author's intellectual property. If you would like permission to use material from the book (other than for review purposes), please contact the publisher. Thank you for your support of the author's rights.

Yen On
150 West 30th Street, 19th Floor
New York, NY 10001

Visit us at yenpress.com • facebook.com/yenpress • twitter.com/yenpress
yenpress.tumblr.com • instagram.com/yenpress

First Yen On Edition: November 2022
Edited by Yen On Editorial: Maya Deutsch
Designed by Yen Press Design: Liz Parlett

Yen On is an imprint of Yen Press, LLC.
The Yen On name and logo are trademarks of Yen Press, LLC.

The publisher is not responsible for websites (or their content) that are not owned by the publisher.

Library of Congress Cataloging-in-Publication Data
Names: Akizakura, Hiroro, author. | Dangmill, illustrator. | Piatkowska, Kiki, translator.
Title: Cross-dressing villainess Cecilia Sylvie / Hiroro Akizakura ; illustration by Dangmill ; translation by Kiki Piatkowska.
Other titles: Akuyaku reijo, cecilia sylvie wa shinitakunai. English
Description: First Yen On edition. | New York, NY : Yen On, 2021. | Audience: Ages 13+ |
Summary: Reincarnated as a villainess in a video game, Cecilia avoids her death flag by masquerading as a man, cross-dressing and assuming a new identity, trying not to let her guise slip with the prince.
Identifiers: LCCN 2021039071 | ISBN 9781975334215 (v. 1 ; trade paperback) |
ISBN 9781975334239 (v. 2 ; trade paperback) | ISBN 9781975342920 (v. 3 ; trade paperback)
Subjects: CYAC: Fantasy. | Male impersonators—Fiction. | Video games—Fiction. |
Secrets—Fiction. | Princes—Fiction. | LCGFT: Fantasy fiction. | Light novels.
Classification: LCC PZ7.1.A3927 Cr 2021 | DDC [Fic]—dc23
LC record available at https://lccn.loc.gov/2021039071

ISBNs: 978-1-9753-4292-0 (paperback)
978-1-9753-4293-7 (ebook)

10 9 8 7 6 5 4 3 2 1

LSC-C

Printed in the United States of America

CONTENTS

Name: Cecilia Sylvie

Gilbert Sylvie

Cecilia's younger adoptive brother and a love interest in the game. Helps her pose as a boy at school.

Oscar Abel Prosper

Crown prince. Cecilia's fiancé and a love interest in the game

Cecilia Sylvie

Daughter of Duke Sylvie. A villainess who appears in *Holy Maiden of Vleugel Academy 3*.

Cecil Admina

Cecilia's male alter ego, the son of a baron. Known as the school prince.

Cross-Dressing Villainess Cecilia Sylvie 3

Characters

Jade Benjamin

A young merchant. Cecilia's classmate and a love interest in the game.

Lean Rhazaloa

A daughter to a baron. The protagonist of *Holy Maiden of Vleugel Academy 3*.

Eins Machias

A love interest in the game. Strong-minded but very caring toward his twin brother.

Zwei Machias

A love interest in the game. Somewhat timid.

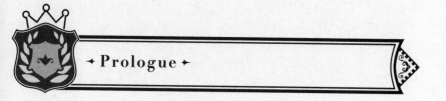

In the beginning, the world was ruled by demons. Dark haze perpetually blocked the sunlight, and crops would not grow. What little sources of water there were kept drying up. People barely clung to sanity. Starving beasts lost their fear of the humans and attacked them out of desperation, and wars raged to no end. The hostile environment relentlessly culled the human population.

But then, the goddess descended from the heavens to save them. Together with the sovereign, to whom all humans pledged their allegiance, she fought the demons for seven days and seven nights. Eventually, she succeeded at driving them into the subterranean depths and sealing them there.

Though banished, the possibility remained that the demons would break the seal and return one day. To prevent them from running rampant again, the goddess appointed the child born from her union with the human king as a Holy Maiden who would protect the land, assisted by seven knights entrusted with the seven spirits who served the goddess.

So went the legend of the Holy Maiden and her knights, passed down through the generations in the Kingdom of Prosper.

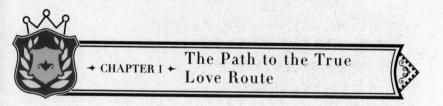

Vleugel Academy had its very own prince.

Honey-blond hair framed his face with eyes like dazzling sapphires, porcelain-white complexion, a dainty nose, and shapely lips. His sweet voice was music to the ears, and his smile was not just charming, but bewitchingly beautiful.

The fact that the color of his uniform had changed from white to black did not even slightly blemish his powerful charisma.

"Um, what happened to your uniform…?"

A group of blushing girls, confused by their school prince's getup, appeared behind him. He spun around to face his admirers with a flourish of his full-length black cape.

Beneath the cape, which had an upturned collar, he wore a burgundy vest. His cravat, fluffed up to look bigger than usual, was fastened with a square ruby of the same color. Instead of the usual uniform slacks, he wore a pair of tightly fitted pants, which amplified the long and slender appearance of his legs. Dressed in this manner, he looked like a supernatural creature from folklore—a vampire.

"Do I look silly in this?"

"N-no, not at all! You're... You're even more..."

Her cheeks flushing an even deeper shade of red, the girl who had said that glanced bashfully down at her feet. Seeing her squirming with embarrassment awoke the prince's sense of mischief. Grinning so as to expose the sharp tips of his canines, he drew her close and whispered into her ear.

"Perhaps you'd like me to bite into that pretty little neck of yours and have a sip of your blood?"

"H-huh? B-bite me?!"

The prince released the girl, who looked so hot and bothered that steam was practically escaping from her ears. Seeing that his prank had achieved the desired effect, the prince smiled playfully.

"Just joking!"

The girl was so confused by the whirlwind of emotions she was experiencing that her legs buckled. A chorus of high-pitched squeals rose up around them.

The prince was named Cecil Admina.

Clad in a vampire outfit, the male alter ego of Duke Sylvie's cross-dressing daughter was proving even more irresistible to her female classmates.

"Sorry about that. Are you okay?"

"Y-yes..."

Cecil helped the girl back to her feet. She stood up unsteadily like a newborn fawn. The gaggle of girls who'd witnessed the scene rushed to her side to escort her away.

"Are you all right?!"

"Snap out of it!"

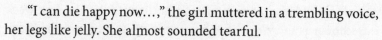

"I can die happy now...," the girl muttered in a trembling voice, her legs like jelly. She almost sounded tearful.

Maybe I shouldn't have done that...

Cecil only wanted to fluster the girl a little, make her blush a bit or giggle. He hadn't been expecting anything this dramatic.

She'd probably be gutted if she found out I'm a girl.

He smiled bitterly, feeling somewhat guilty.

Cecil was actually a girl from the modern world who had been transmigrated into a dating sim—*Holy Maiden of Vleugel Academy 3*—as Cecilia Sylvie, daughter of Duke Sylvie and the doomed villainess of the game. She was cross-dressing as a boy at school to escape the cruel fate that otherwise lay in store for her.

"I came to see what the commotion was, and of course, it had to be you stirring up trouble again."

Cecilia turned around upon hearing a familiar voice. It was Oscar. Judging by his glare of disapproval, he must have seen at least part of what happened. The crown prince was a full head taller than her. He looked her up and down quizzically.

"What is this you're wearing? Does it have to do with preparations for Advent?"

"Um, yeah, you hit the nail on the head. Lean insisted on it..."

"Not again..."

Oscar frowned in exasperation, perhaps remembering the *qipao* episode. Cecilia scratched her cheek, not sure what to say.

Advent was an annual holiday celebrating the goddess' visit to the world of mortals. It was observed on a huge scale in the Kingdom of Prosper and included festivities modeled after the legend of the goddess coming down from the heavens to seal away the evil demons. The holiday spanned two weeks, with the presumed day of the goddess' advent landing in the middle. The first week was known as the Week of Ashes, while the second was the Week of Light.

During the Week of Ashes, the custom was for people to dress up as demons and spooky monsters to represent the time when those foul creatures still ruled the land. Conversely, the tradition for the Week of Light festivities was white outfits symbolizing the goddess.

As harvest celebrations were moved to coincide with Advent, it became the most important holiday in the Kingdom of Prosper, with the pivotal day falling on October 31. To put it simply, this was the game's Halloween event.

It's the middle of September, so we still have a whole month to go...
Cecilia let out a sigh, digging through the memories of her past life yet again. Advent is a popular in-game event where the love interests appear in outfits different from their usual attire. It's also an important opportunity to score affection points. Reaching a certain level of intimacy with a love interest triggers a date where you can walk around together, checking out what the festival has to offer. Since she'd replayed this part many times to see all the different outcomes for each love interest, Cecilia remembered Advent very well.

But most people aren't dressing up for the Halloween event like this.

She pinched the sides of her cape. *Holy Maiden of Vleugel Academy 3* was a dating sim for girls set in a fantasy realm based on European aristocracies of yore. Sure, legends about werewolves and vampires existed in this world, but the characters' event outfits were mostly based on cute fairy tales. No one wears anything resembling Cecilia's costume in the game. So why was she dressed like a vampire, totally out of line with the game's original aesthetic?

That was thanks to none other than Lean Rhazaloa, gamebreaker supreme.

You weren't originally one of the knights, Cecilia, so there's no set Halloween outfit for you. Which means I get to unleash my creativity and make you one, right?!
Let's go all out for Halloween!

She'd set to her task with unbridled enthusiasm and made the costume on a treadle sewing machine.

By the way, Lean had already forced Cecilia to model in that vampire outfit and sketched her...so she could use the drawings as illustrations in her next novel.

"So that's what happened... But why are you wearing the costume now? Advent is still a long way off. You're bound to attract attention dressed like this for no apparent reason."

Oscar was still staring at her with consternation. Cecilia laughed awkwardly.

"I know, but Lean wanted to make sure it was actually wearable, so she asked me to walk around in it for a bit. I thought I'd get weird looks if I went into the schoolhouse in it, so I stayed outside, but my fans spotted me," Cecilia said, feigning resignation.

Oscar let out a long sigh.

"You have no common sense. All you had to do was try it on in your room. There's no need to prance around in it outside. How could you have expected to go unnoticed?"

"I had some errands to run. Look, I won't stand out so much without this."

She took off the cape and folded it over her arm. Now she could easily pass for a young aristocrat in formal wear.

"This doesn't look outlandish at all, right?"

"I suppose it doesn't. So where were you going?"

"To see Grace. I need to get something done today."

Cecilia started walking away, and Oscar followed, even though he'd just come from that direction. Maybe he'd decided to keep her company. She noticed he kept stealing glances at the cloak she was carrying.

"I must say, Lean is a skilled seamstress. The foreign outfit you were wearing that other time was also her work, wasn't it?"

"Yeah, she's good at this sort of thing! But she's a bit too much of a perfectionist, if you ask me."

"Really?"

"Uh-huh."

Cecilia nodded and produced two fluffy objects from one of her pockets.

"What's this?"

"Wolf ears, no?"

Oscar craned his neck to get a better look at the items in Cecilia's hand. Keeping her gaze on them, Cecilia continued her explanation.

"You see, at first, Lean wanted to dress me up as a werewolf, not a vampire. But I had her give up on that idea—it would be way too embarrassing, don't you think? She was going to throw them out because they 'didn't come out quite right,' but I rescued them from being sent to the trash!"

"You rescued them, huh? But whatever are you going to do with them?"

"Hmm... Maybe I'll wear them?"

The ears didn't have clips, so Cecilia just held them to her head. She glanced up at Oscar.

"Do you think they look good on me?"

Seeing her looking up at him bashfully, Oscar stopped in his tracks like he'd been struck by lightning. He dropped his head and raised a hand to his face as if to cover his eyes.

"You look like a cat..."

"Huh?"

"Nothing."

He started walking again. For some reason, his cheeks seemed a bit flushed.

"That will do, Oscar."

They'd arrived at the research lab. Cecilia turned to face Oscar and gave him a smile, the towering building just behind her.

"I guess you ended up walking me all the way here. Thanks!"

"Don't mention it. Anyway, do you need to see Grace about something?"

"That's right. I'm hoping she might help me out," she replied brightly, ready to depart. Before she could, however, Oscar paused as if mulling something over before speaking to her again.

"Do you mind if I go in with you, Cecil?"

"Huh? But why?"

She opened her eyes wide and tilted her head, puzzled. Perhaps Oscar wasn't expecting her to throw a question back at him, because he averted his gaze and trailed off evasively.

"Um... Sorry, Oscar! But I want to discuss this with Grace in private."

"It's not for my ears, either?"

"Well... No. Sorry."

Cecilia dropped her eyes apologetically, and Oscar nodded, deciding not to pursue it further. Still, she did notice he was gritting his teeth.

What's up with him?

Come to think of it, he'd been acting oddly all day. He gave off that "got something to say but can't spit it out" vibe. It was making things more and more awkward.

"Oscar, is something on your mi—?"

"I'll leave you here and head back, then."

"Oh, okay."

He cut her off and turned around to head back the way they'd came, giving her one last look before leaving. There was a strange, big-brotherly warmth in his eyes.

"Make sure to come back before it gets late."

"Yeah, sure! You don't need to worry about me!"

"I don't know where you get that confidence from…"

He looked at her skeptically. Cecilia thumped her chest.

"I haven't been training for nothing! If anyone tries to attack me, they're done for!"

"I think you're overestimating yourself…"

"Besides, Gil's coming to meet up with me."

"…I see."

He nodded, then said his good-byes, and left after making an odd pause. Cecilia followed him with her eyes as he went, so confused there might as well have been a question mark above her head.

I swear he was holding back a question. Does he think something's up with me?

He certainly appeared to be acting that way, but Cecilia couldn't really think of anything suspicious about herself. She worried for a second that he might have found out she was really a girl, but that seemed rather unlikely after she'd managed to fool him through that risky cottage room-sharing event.

Meh, it's not like I can read his mind!

Cecilia saw no point in wasting energy fretting over things she couldn't be certain of. That quality of hers could be advantageous, but it could also bite her in the butt.

She turned and started walking toward the lab building, unaware that Oscar had stopped to watch her.

"…So what do you think I should do in this situation, Grace?"

"Why don't you just become the Holy Maiden?"

Cecilia slumped despondently at the curt reply. Grace was too absorbed in her work to so much as glance at her.

Cecilia had come to the lab to pick Grace's brain. In her past life, she'd finished all the routes in the game.

As it stood, none of the Holy Maiden candidates actually wanted to occupy the position. The thing was, though, Cecilia had inadvertently scored a Sacred Artifact—Gilbert's. Left like this, the bad end of the game would trigger, and Cecilia would die. But she wasn't going to just resign herself to that fate. She raised her head and stepped closer to Grace.

"I won't do it! It would put my life in danger!"

"You're making that assumption based on what happens in the game, but your actions have already caused the events here to diverge from the original scenario. You becoming Holy Maiden won't necessarily lead to the same ending as it does in the game."

"That's a fair point, but it doesn't mean that it's out of the question, either!"

"Well...I supposed that's true."

Cecilia's reasonable objection seemed to finally get through to Grace, who sighed and looked at her directly for the first time since she got here. Though it was obvious she found Cecilia bothersome, she was not entirely unwilling to help.

Grace pointed her index finger at Cecilia.

"If you want my advice, give me a concrete problem to solve."

"What...?"

"Is your end goal to avoid becoming Holy Maiden? Preventing your death? I can't work with general concepts like that. Give me something more immediate and concrete as a starting point."

Cecilia frowned, put off by the other girl's rigid scientific reasoning. She thought for a moment.

"Can it be something not very realistic?"

"Shoot."

"I'd like to somehow make the Obstructions go away."

It had occurred to her earlier—if the Obstructions disappeared, there'd be no need for Holy Maidens in the first place. Not that she thought it really was within the realm of possibility for her to do anything about these creatures or things or spirits or whatever they were.

"That's easy."

Cecilia blinked, wondering if she misheard.

"You'll have to trigger the True Love route."

"That will make them disappear?"

"It should make it possible to achieve that, yes."

Grace smiled confidently and explained that in the True Love ending, everyone bands together to banish the Obstructions.

"You achieve this outcome by raising all the love interests' affection to a certain level, getting an artifact from every knight, and being recognized as a Holy Maiden candidate."

"I don't think I can do that..."

There was no way she could pull that off, Cecilia realized, her face falling. She'd been dressing up as a boy this whole time to avoid becoming a Holy Maiden candidate. And how could she even dream of collecting all the Sacred Artifacts at this stage? If she came forward as a candidate and revealed she was really a girl at this point, it would definitely upset quite a few people for a variety of reasons.

Grace gave her a fleeting smile.

"Don't worry. Your appearance won't be a problem."

"What do you mean?"

"You don't have to get the True Love ending."

Cecilia tilted her head at this contradictory statement.

"I said you'd have to *trigger* the True Love route, not that you'd have to see it through. It might be impossible to get the normal True Love ending after you've messed up the storyline so much."

"So I have to trigger the True Love flag without making it all the way to the ending?"

Grace nodded.

"To get rid of the Obstructions once and for all, you'll have to enter the shrine where the current Holy Maiden resides."

"Why is that?"

"There are several reasons, but the main one is that you need an item from there to exorcise the Obstructions. Activating the True Love flag is a requirement for entry. But once you get that item, there's no need to continue with that ending."

This was all news to Cecilia, who listened with widened eyes to Grace's matter-of-fact explanation.

"You don't need the artifacts to trigger the route, either. The only prerequisite is reaching a certain affection level with every single love interest. Get close with everyone, and you'll unlock it."

"With...everyone? Including Eins and Zwei?"

"They're also love interests in the game, so that goes without saying."

"Right..."

Cecilia mumbled an unenthusiastic reply. Grace was puzzled by this.

"What's wrong? Normally, you'd say something along the lines of *Right, I'm on it!* and shoot out of the room like a supercharged bundle of energy."

"You're making me sound so simple-minded..."

"Well, you don't exactly give off the impression of being someone with a high IQ."

"Huuuh?"

Grace's candid put-down threw Cecilia off.

"That's just my personal opinion, so feel free to disregard it," Grace added, as if it would make her quip sting less.

"Anyway, why the long face? Did the twins' route give you trouble in your past life?"

"I didn't even try to complete them..."

"Why not?"

Cecilia suddenly grew evasive.

"You know… Their endings are bad… I don't really like that sort of stuff."

"Ah, right. I take it you weren't interested in seeing the Confinement and Lovers' Suicide endings?"

Grace gave her an understanding look. Cecilia nodded gravely.

Eins and Zwei were sons of Marquis Machias. Though they were identical twins, you could easily tell them apart by their personalities—one was stubborn and confident, while the other was shy and timid. Their characterization in the game is rather simple, but the fact that they get along so well suggests they are deeper than they initially appear. Cecilia's past self, Hiyono, had been looking forward to completing the twins' routes…until she came across a piece of unsettling content on social media.

It was a fan-made manga by an artist who'd finished their routes before her. Though the work itself was of high quality, the real issue was what happens in it. Titled *After the Bad Ending*, it concerns Eins imprisoning Lean and keeping her as his pet…

Hiyono had screamed when she saw it. It wasn't just that she was upset about spoilers; the narrative also disturbed her. She couldn't get it out of her mind, so she did some research online and read up on the bad endings you get by romancing the twins.

Their upbringing had caused them to become morbidly codependent, so raising the affections of one in lieu of the other causes the scorned twin to become fanatically jealous, resulting in some terrible endings. They were rather twisted, too. If Eins is left out while the player romances his brother, he goes mad with jealousy and locks Lean up. This is the Confinement ending. In Zwei's case, he keeps third-wheeling until the unlucky pair eventually commit suicide. That constitutes the Lovers' Suicide ending.

In reality, the player can only complete their romance routes through carefully raising both of their affection stats simultaneously. Clearing their route is almost like doing a high-wire act, which was why the fans dubbed them the "Tightrope Twins."

The warped brothers must have had their appeal, because there was far more fan art based on their bad endings than there was of the happy ones.

They weren't up Hiyono's alley, though. In fact, she really despised those endings. That's why she'd never completed the brothers' routes in the game, and she hadn't wanted to have anything to do with them here, either.

"A bad ending like Dante's, where you get killed abruptly, doesn't bother me so much, but I can't stand disturbing stuff."

"I know what you mean. The twins' endings are on a whole other level of bad. But their routes are easier than Dante's. Anyway, you don't have to actually trigger their endings, so I wouldn't worry so much about them."

"I guess…," Cecilia replied quietly, voice quivering. Thinking about those chilling events made her feel awful. She was getting goose bumps just imagining the possibility of those horrible things being done to her.

"This is the only way of getting rid of the Obstructions. If you don't want to deal with the twins, you'll have to abandon that ambition."

"I don't want to do either…"

"You'll have to decide on one or the other."

Grace returned to the work on her desk, making it clear that, as far as she was concerned, the discussion was over. She'd already started busily scanning some research papers. Cecilia got the hint and stood up to thank her and leave, but before she went out the door, Grace called out to her.

"Do be careful. I wouldn't want you to get hurt."

She smiled with a kindness Cecilia had never seen in her before.

"Go out there and change your fate. I hope you can do it."

Grace's encouraging words did the trick, and Cecilia brightened up. To say the other girl was emotionally reserved would be an understatement, but she was trying her best to show that she was rooting for Cecilia. It warmed her heart.

"I'll try! Thanks, Grace!"

"No worries."

Grace smiled briefly and directed her gaze at the door.

"Your friend's here."

"Huh?"

"I can recognize people by their footsteps."

No sooner had she said that than they heard a knock.

"Come in."

The door opened a crack and a familiar face peered inside.

"I came to get Cecil. Ready to go?"

It was Gilbert.

"Sure!"

Cecilia nodded emphatically, filled with energy once again.

One week later...

"Are you kidding? You're going to walk the tightrope again?"

"I've got to. Sorry...," Cecilia said apologetically.

She heard Gilbert sigh from behind the door.

Cecilia was in the dorm that day. Gilbert was waiting for her outside her room while she was getting ready, putting a new jacket on.

"I've thought about it lots and lots, and this seems like the best option."

"Removing all Obstructions once and for all?"

"Yeah. The things I have to do for it don't sit well with me, either, but I've got to make it happen. I'm sorry for worrying you..."

"Never mind me. Being anxious about you is pretty much my natural state now."

Cecilia giggled guiltily, hearing a note of resignation in Gilbert's voice. She felt sorry for him, but she had to tackle the Obstructions at this point, or there'd be no future for her. She was going to talk to Eins and Zwei to get started.

She styled her wig with more care than usual, straightened her collar, and took one last look at herself in the mirror.

"All good!"

Cecil Admina, son of a baron, was staring back at her in formal wear. She'd had this official-looking outfit prepared before entering the academy to use for events where she'd need to look impressive but not as showy, like soirees.

She opened the door and joined Gilbert, who was also in formal attire, with half of his bangs smoothed back. The black of his clothes matched that of his hair.

"Ready to go?"

"Yup!"

They headed out of the dorm together.

In the game, Lean meets the twins at the Vleugel Academy spring tea party. The students of Vleugel Academy were all nobility who would one day hold significant political influence, and the fancy tea parties, organized in spring and fall, presented an opportunity for them to socialize. While attendance wasn't required, very few would let this chance to forge useful connections for the future slip by.

Lean comes to the party at Cecilia's behest, but when she makes her appearance in her usual school uniform instead of a dress, she becomes an object of ridicule for Cecilia and her clique. The villainess had invited Lean knowing full well that she neither had the appropriate outfit nor was aware of the etiquette for this sort of gathering. That's right—Cecilia intended to make her the subject of mockery all along.

Just as the inexperienced Lean looks down at her feet to hide the tears welling in her eyes, not even fully understanding why the high-born girls are laughing at her, the gallant Machias brothers make their entrance. They take Lean under their wings and reproach Cecilia.

"You should be ashamed."

"Someone as vain and superficial as you is in no position to criticize her."

Furious at their impertinence, Cecilia leaves, her face bright red with shame. The boys then turn their attention to Lean, who is utterly bewildered.

"Are you all right?"

"Why don't we find somewhere to sit down together?"

From then on, their bond begins to deepen.

This was the event Cecilia was trying to recreate now, only it would be at the fall tea party, rather than the spring one.

"Getting to meet the twins is the tricky part. I can't make a bad first impression by bullying Lean to trigger the event…"

"I'm sure you'll come up with something. But first, tell me where Eins keeps the heroine locked up, and give me all the info you have on Zwei's Lovers' Suicide ending, too."

Cecilia blinked.

"Hey, Gil… You're not assuming I'm going to fail, are you?"

Gilbert gave her a glacial stare.

"Think back to all that has happened recently and ask yourself how successful your plans have been. Still feeling so confident about this one?"

"Well, um…"

In the span of less than half a year, Cecilia had already made countless blunders. Gilbert was privy to them all; no wonder he was wary about her new scheme.

"You're just too impulsive to think things through."

"I guess that's true…"

"And you always make these big decisions without consulting me."

"Can't deny that either…"

"You only loop me in after you've already made up your mind or set things in motion, and you expect me to play a supporting role in your plans."

"Uh…"

"Honestly, I ask myself how I can like someone like you at least once a week."

"I'm sorry it always turns out that way, Gil…"

Cecilia looked deflated as her brother chastised her. But then he turned away from her and forced a smile.

"Never mind. I'm used to being your pawn."

"Gil, I—"

"You see now where I'm coming from, right? So give me all the details you have. We can't let you wind up imprisoned or forced to commit suicide. Did Grace tell you anything?"

At Gilbert's insistence, Cecilia laid out everything she knew to him, adding that she'd learned most of this from Grace, since she hadn't completed those routes in her past life.

"By the way, Gil, how come you accepted everything I told you about my past life at face value?"

They had just reached the plaza between the boys' and girls' dormitories. Gilbert turned to face Cecilia when she stopped abruptly.

"Are you saying I should have accused you of lying?"

"No, but… If I were you, I'd have found it hard to believe."

Gilbert gave her statement some thought, stroking his chin.

"I sensed there was something odd about you long before that."

"Like what?"

"Like how you predicted your betrothal to the prince when you were six years old."

"Huh? I did that?"

"Yeah. Nobody knew if it would be you or the Wills girl at the time."

Now that he mentioned it, maybe Cecilia said it would be her back then. If she'd been six, that meant Gilbert was only five. His memory was no joke.

"And when Donny came to our house for the first time, you knew his name even before he introduced himself."

"Really?"

"And you were always going on about weird stuff, like how you wanted to eat 'instant noodles' or how you wished you had your 'smartphone.' Then one day, totally out of the blue, you demanded that Hans train you. When I asked why, you told me, 'Because I don't want to die!' That made me so confused."

"Ha-ha-ha, I can imagine!"

Her laughter was a bit strained. She knew she could be ditzy at times, but she hadn't realized it was this bad.

"You had lots of other weird moments like that, too. I was sure you had some strange secret. But I won't lie, when you revealed it all to me and said you'd be posing as a guy at school to save your life, I did think for a moment that you'd gone crazy."

He looked exhausted. Cecilia smiled awkwardly.

"It must have been quite a shock to you…"

"You think? It made me pretty mad."

"What? Why?"

"Because I thought some jerk must have been messing with you, telling you all that nonsense."

Cecilia opened her eyes wide in surprise.

"Hang on, Gil... Are you saying you didn't believe me when I told you about being transmigrated?"

"Of course I didn't! Would you believe someone if they started spinning you a yarn about their bizarre recollections of a past life? Especially if it was coming from the naivest person you knew? I was sure it was all a fib."

Cecilia was so flustered by this revelation that her lower lip quivered. Gilbert ignored that.

"But things kept playing out as you said they would, so now you've got me convinced, I guess."

It sounded like he'd only started believing her recently, as though he'd been playing along and assuming she was freaking out over nothing earlier.

"You've been helping me all this time even though you didn't believe me?"

"Yeah."

"Why?"

Gilbert had enrolled Cecilia at the academy, helped create her alter ego, supplied her with a boy's school uniform, and had done a ton of other things for her. But if he didn't believe her life was at risk, then why had he gone to such lengths to help her?

"Because you wanted me to."

Cecilia tilted her head in confusion at his matter-of-fact reply.

"If you told me you wanted to attend the academy dressed as a boy without explaining why, I'd have helped you all the same. Regardless of whether I sensed there was something unusual about you."

"Really?"

"I have a soft spot for you. Say the word, and I'll move mountains for you."

He said it so nonchalantly that Cecilia laughed, assuming he was just being sarcastic. Suddenly, they heard a familiar high-pitched voice from behind.

"I'm sorry if I kept you waiting."

They turned around to find Lean in a dress. It wasn't the kind you'd wear to a soiree, with a décolletage, but a more modest one fastened at the neck. Cecilia had supplied it to her, along with an invitation to the party.

I've got to check as many boxes as I can to trigger the event...

Lean looked around to make sure they were alone, then relaxed the stoic expression she wore as the game's protagonist to that of Cecilia's trusted friend.

"Getting ready was so frustrating. They should've hired more helpers for the occasion!"

The formal dresses the girls were expected to wear for the party were quite a hassle to put on, so the female students had to get help from either maids employed by the academy or their families. Lean had needed to ask for an academy servant to help her out because of her familial circumstances, but as there were so few of them, it was a rather long wait.

Seeing Lean in a dress for the first time, Cecilia exclaimed:

"Wow! It looks amazing on you! You're so cute!"

"Right? Cute is my middle name!"

Lean really was adorable. So endearing, in fact, that it was impossible to begrudge her for bragging about it.

Lean glanced over at Gilbert.

"Don't hold back with the compliments."

"You want me to flatter you? Then try saying something deserving of praise."

The air between them turned frigid. Cecilia looked from one to the other with concern in her eyes.

"Why is it so hard for you to think of something nice to say to a lady? Gloomy men are unpopular for a reason."

"Why do you care? And sorry, but I can't stand people who feel entitled to compliments just because they exist."

"That's enough! Why do you have to argue all the time?" Cecilia butted in to stop them. Lean and Gilbert had been at odds with each other ever since Cecilia revealed to Gilbert that she was her best friend from her past life who'd also been transmigrated as a game character. The two had rarely interacted before then, but at least they hadn't been fighting. That being said, it was nice they could be their real selves around each other now.

"He's always trying to get on my nerves, that's why."

"I don't see a single reason why my sister would like you."

"Stop already! Don't make me choose between you two, because I can't!"

Cecilia put her hands on her head dramatically, but her friends just stared at her with resignation.

"No one's making you choose, dummy," Lean said.

"Who you're friends with is your own business," Gilbert added.

Aren't they actually alike in some ways?

Despite their arguing, they would often wind up saying the exact same thing.

Lean must have had enough of talking to Gilbert, because she hiked up the skirt of her dress and turned toward the academy courtyard.

"This favor is going to cost you, Cecilia."

"Charge me what you will…"

Lean smiled at Cecilia's meek reply.

"Okay, my prince. Let's clear the twins' route."

"Ha-ha… Ready when you are."

Lean gave Cecilia her hand, and they walked off together.

→ CHAPTER 2 → The Tightrope Twins

Vleugel Academy's tea parties were held in the courtyard. Surrounded by the majestic buildings on campus, the area featured a lush lawn, perfectly spaced trees, and cute semicircular flower beds of zinnias in full bloom. In the center of the yard sat a fountain—a symbol of wealth—shooting water up high, and at the sides were two gazebos and four stone statues, presumably depicting past counts of House Clemence who'd served as headmasters of the academy.

Cecilia and Lean weaved through the crowd of young nobles crowded around circular tables. It wasn't the kind of gathering where you sat down to enjoy your food and drink, but rather one where you nibbled here and there as you ambled along, chatting about worldly matters or business.

Cecilia craned her neck and looked every which way, trying to spot Eins and Zwei.

"I've never been to a party like this. Everyone seems so earnest."

"Of course they are. Not everyone's family has as secure a social position as House Sylvie does. Many students are hoping to make connections with future heads of influential families or are looking to find a suitable marriage candidate."

On closer inspection, the attendees seemed more serious and

engaged here than they were in class. Cecilia had heard that some girls enrolled at Vleugel specifically for the tea parties—she had been incredulous of that until now.

"The only people who can afford to relax are heirs to family titles and wealth. On the other hand, there's a lot at stake here for the girls who have yet to be engaged, along with the second, third, and later sons of noble houses. They're desperate to secure their future by talking to the right people... Oh, it seems that Gilbert's not having the best of times."

Cecilia looked toward where Lean was pointing. Her brother had attracted a crowd. No sooner had they entered the courtyard than girls started swarming him. To a casual observer, it would seem that he was calmly allowing them to engage him in conversation, but those who knew him could recognize that he was in fact growing distressed. Similar groups of girls surrounding firstborn sons of influential families had also formed.

"That was to be expected, especially now that House Coulson's planning to take him back."

"What?!"

"A young gentleman with strong connections to two duchies— what a catch! That's why all these girls are trying to impress him. The general public is not aware of his issues with the Coulsons."

"Is he really going back to them?!"

Lean blinked, surprised at the note of panic in Cecilia's voice.

"Wait, you didn't know?"

"No! Gil hasn't told me a thing!" Cecilia exclaimed, flustered.

Lean raised an index finger and preceded her explanation with a disclaimer that it was just a rumor she'd heard.

"We caught Bernard, and Ticky's wrongdoings were exposed soon after that, so neither are a viable second choice after Nichol."

"And that's why they want Gil back?"

"That's what some people are saying. Everybody knows that Nichol Coulson is in poor health. He's also famously accomplished, of course, but don't you think his family would want to have an able-bodied potential heir on standby just in case?"

If that was true, then the Coulson family was utterly selfish. How craven of them to put Gilbert up for adoption when they had no use for him, only to request his return when it was convenient for them.

"On top of that, several students have seen Mrs. Coulson around the academy, and it wasn't just a one-off. Jade thinks she might have been coming here to talk with Gilbert directly."

"I didn't know that…," Cecilia muttered, thrown by the new information.

That explains why he's been disappearing after classes lately…

She'd actually invited Gilbert to come along with her to speak with Grace the other day, confident that he'd readily agree as usual, but he claimed he had something else to do that day. While that was atypical of him, she didn't think much of it at the time. In retrospect, perhaps he'd been meeting with Mrs. Coulson that day.

I wonder what Gil wants to do…

Though his parents had wanted him out of the way, they were still his parents. If, and this was a big "if," Gilbert earnestly asked them to let him return to the family, they would certainly grant him their permission. The choice was all his.

I'd miss him…

It wasn't Cecilia's place to try to persuade him to stay in her family, though. If it made him happy to be finally acknowledged by his biological parents, then she ought to rejoice as well. In any case, she was only his adoptive sister, so her views on what he should do didn't really matter.

"Anyway, what do you want to do now? Mock me, like in the game?"

"Huh?"

Cecilia had been so absorbed in her thoughts that for a moment she had no idea what Lean was talking about. The other girl put her hands on her hips and gave her a pointed look.

"Aren't we here so that you can meet the twins?"

"Ah, right!"

The matter of Gilbert distracted her so much that she'd completely forgotten what she was here for. She had to focus.

"Um, I think following the game script is too risky. Botching our first impression would only make it harder to garner the twins' affection."

"Yeah, I was thinking the same thing."

"Besides, I'd have no idea what to tease you about anyway."

Unlike in the game, where she shows up in her school uniform, Lean was wearing an appropriate dress for the event. Cecilia couldn't see a single thing about her friend's outfit that could give rise to ridicule. Plus, she wasn't particularly good at picking up on people's weaknesses. Lean smiled at her stumped friend.

"Bullying just isn't in your character, is it? Do you have another plan?"

"I haven't thought that far…"

They looked at each other, both without ideas. Then someone approached them…

"Well, well. Look who came to the gathering."

Cecilia twitched and looked up to find Oscar in his finery.

"Oscar?! What are you doing here?"

"I always attend the tea parties."

Oscar's outfit was the opposite of Gilbert's—entirely white. Coincidentally, it was similar to the outfit he'd worn at the soiree where Cecilia first met him. And he wasn't alone, either…

"Heya!"

"Dante's here, too!"

He was also dressed formally. Cecilia had never seen him showing so little skin. He really was looking rather elegant. You wouldn't think twice if he claimed to be a young aristocrat.

"I was under the impression you'd rather avoid this kind of function…"

"Well, Oscar's an easy target at social gatherings, so I'm keeping him company."

"You're his bodyguard?"

"Nah, I wouldn't go so far as to call myself that. I'm here just because I don't want anyone else besides me laying their filthy hands on my precious prince."

Dante gave a hearty chuckle. Ever since his true identity had been revealed, he'd dropped the act and was having quite a lot of fun just being himself. In the game, he conceals his true nature from Oscar until the very end, so the player never gets a chance to see how casual and carefree he can be.

Unamused, Oscar peeled off Dante's arm from his neck.

"I told him he didn't need to come…"

"But here I am. Besides, there've been some worrying stories going around recently."

"What stories?"

Cecilia was drawing a blank. Dante replied in a slightly lowered voice.

"About Prince Janis being up to something again."

Janis was a ruler from a neighboring country who'd sent Dante to assassinate Oscar. Cecilia knew him as the last boss of the Oscar, Gilbert, and Dante routes.

"There's no reason to put stock into those rumors," Oscar asserted.

"But they're about the dude who sent me to kill you. Better safe than sorry," Dante replied.

"You have no proof he's really plotting anything."

"If I had obeyed him, you'd be kissing daisies by now."

"That's not funny."

"Neither are you, but I like you that way."

Dante laughed at Oscar's grimace.

There weren't many people in the prince's vicinity, and it seemed like Dante was intent on keeping it that way. It went against etiquette to interrupt two nobles seemingly engrossed in conversation.

"And why are you standing here as if you are lost?"

Oscar's question reminded Cecilia of what she had come for.

"We're trying to find someone we want to make friends with!"

"Who would that be?"

"The Machias twins. Do you know them?"

Oscar raised an eyebrow.

"I do. I'm acquainted with all the noble families."

"I should've guessed. Maybe you could help us meet them!"

"We don't even know where they are," Lean added helplessly.

Oscar sized them up.

"Do you want me to introduce you?"

"Huh?"

"I can just lead you to them and present you. I've seen the Machiases walking around a short while ago, so they must still be nearby."

"You'll do that for us? Thanks!"

Cecilia joyously threw her arms up in the air, to which Oscar gave a brief, puzzled smile.

"Why is it so important that you make friends with them?"

"Why do you ask?"

"There has to be a reason."

"Um...," Cecilia muttered indistinctly. She didn't know what to tell him. Oscar was still being kept in the dark about the fact that she was cross-dressing and that she remembered her past life, so she couldn't tell him the real reason.

Why is he asking anyway?

He'd been acting suspicious of her since last week. Was he on the verge of unveiling her secret?

The thought of it triggered a flashback of a screen from the game, all red with blood. Cecilia turned pale.

"Y-you know what, thanks. But I think we'll find them without your help!"

"Hold on!"

"You saw them over there? Thanks for the info!"

"L-Lord Cecil, wait up!"

But Cecilia, in a great haste to get away from Oscar, wasn't about to wait for Lean.

Oscar stared at his fiancée, who was running away from him at a sprint. When she disappeared in the crowd, he sighed, his heart heavy with unspeakable loneliness.

I knew she wouldn't tell me...

He'd been wise to the fact that Cecil was Cecilia in disguise for some time now and that she had to keep the reason secret from him.

She must be a Holy Maiden candidate.

It had dawned on him recently. That possibility offered the only explanation as to how Cecil had managed to vanquish the Obstruction at the Selection Ceremony and why he possessed a Sacred Artifact. But even though this all made sense to him now, Oscar still felt uneasy. What upset him the most about this situation was that Cecilia didn't trust him enough to tell him this herself.

Oscar touched the Artifact on his wrist. Cecilia must have gotten hers from Gilbert. The mere thought that she trusted Gilbert more than him perturbed him a great deal for some reason.

What is this I'm feeli—?

"Oscar..."

"Hngh?!"

He jumped when he heard someone speak into his ear all of a sudden. Covering his ear as if it hurt, he moved away from the culprit, who shrugged like it was just Oscar being strange.

"Don't moan into my ear like that!"

"You were looking so crestfallen that I had to do something."

Dante put an arm around Oscar's neck and tried to comfort him.

"Don't let it get to you so much. It's nothing personal, I'm sure."

Oscar thought back to when Dante had used "she" to refer to Cecil. It was in late spring, when they were studying for the exams together.

"Do you know Cecil's secret?"

"Hmm. Maybe."

Dante narrowed his eyes as if considering something, before breaking into a smile.

"But I pinky promised not to tell anyone, so I'm afraid I can't tell you either, Oscar."

"And should you be saying that?"

"Whatever do you mean? I haven't told you anything."

He was admitting it in an indirect way. It seemed that Cecilia had sworn Dante to secrecy. Oscar sighed again, looked away from Dante, then listed three names, bending a finger for each one.

"And you're not the only one in the know. Gilbert, Grace, and Lean are as well."

Maybe there were even more people who were aware. It made him depressed to think about it.

"Am I the only one excluded from this secret society?"

He huffed in exasperation.

"I shouldn't have turned down Oscar's offer..."

Cecilia was moping dejectedly after running away from Oscar and Dante. In her mad dash, she seemed to have lost Lean somewhere in the crowd. She'd probably be upset about it.

"Blargh..."

Cecilia hunched her back and sighed.

I bet Oscar thought I was being weird...

She'd panicked and ran away because she was anxious about how he'd acted last week, but come to think of it, his question today wasn't out of the ordinary at all. If you asked someone to introduce you to somebody else, it was only normal that they would want to know why.

I keep thinking of how Oscar is in the game, but he's not like that now...

The Lean-loving hero of the game who wanted to get rid of Cecilia at all costs didn't exist in this world. Nevertheless, Cecilia had internalized this fear of him, which pushed her to act impulsively. But it was unfair of her to be so terrified of him when he hadn't done any harm to her.

"The Oscar in this world doesn't hate Cecilia. He actually likes...her...? Uh...!"

The moment she said this, heat rushed to her face. Memories of the incident at the school infirmary a month earlier came flooding back.

"You're the one I like! Isn't it obvious?!"

But even after that impassioned confession, he continued to treat her like a friend. Cecilia was glad for this since she didn't know how to respond to Oscar, but she couldn't just rely on his goodwill forever while ignoring his feelings.

Another complicating factor was that it wasn't Cecilia who Oscar confessed his love to, but rather her fictional alter ego, Cecil.

This would be easier to deal with if he'd opened up to the real me...

Not that she could think of what to say in that situation, either. She grasped her head in her hands.

I like Oscar, but do I like him in THAT way? I don't have time for romance; my life is at stake here... Oh, hold on...

The cogwheels of her mind jammed for a second.

I was so overwhelmed by my looming death that it didn't sink in at the time but...the way things are heading, am I going to end up marrying Oscar?

"Huuuh...?"

The shock of that realization left her inarticulate for a moment.

"Oscar and I...will get married?"

Now that she'd said it out loud, it finally felt real. Her head started spinning.

What... What... Whaaat?! Wait, so, since he doesn't hate me, he won't annul our engagement. But it's Cecil he's in love with, not me! I mean, I am Cecil, but...

She felt dizzy. Her legs wobbled.

"Whoa!"

She tripped over something. But just as she was about to fall flat on her face, someone caught her in time.

"Are you okay?"

"Huh? Um, yeah..."

When Cecilia raised her head to see who had grabbed her lower torso, she widened her eyes in surprise.

It was a boy of petite build, about the same height as her, wearing a sheepish expression. He had large green eyes with eyelashes so long they gave him a bit of a feminine appearance, and his chestnut-brown hair was braided on the left side. Overall, he gave off a delicate and graceful impression.

Zwei?!

She stopped herself from shouting his name. Zwei checked that she was indeed all right, then told her to take care and left.

I—I found him!

His twin wasn't there, but this was already remarkable progress. She followed after him, taking care not to get noticed.

Cecilia trailed Zwei behind the schoolhouse. There was no one else around, and Zwei appeared to be waiting for someone. Cecilia hid to watch him.

What did he come here for? If he's got nothing better to do, I'd like to talk to him, but it would be suspicious if I showed myself now.

Nobody had any business hanging out behind the schoolhouse when there was a party being held in the courtyard. If he saw her, he would no doubt assume that she'd stalked him. Coming off as a creep would ruin her chances of raising his affection.

I'll go back to where there are more people and find an excuse to chat him up...

"I know you're there. Come out."

She'd already turned to leave but that made her freeze, startled. When had he noticed her?

M-maybe everything will be okay if I come out meekly and introduce myself?

She steeled herself to step out of the shadows...

"I hope you brought what I asked for!"

But that deep voice didn't belong to Zwei. Cecilia crouched again and watched as three students approached Zwei. The burly one in the middle carried himself in a manner that made it glaringly obvious he was a spoiled son of an upstart family. He was flanked by a boy who looked like he was only good for brawling and another who seemed like he took pleasure in bullying others.

A boss and his two goons...

Cecilia frowned, wary of what was going to happen. Zwei took a step toward the other boys.

"I—I did!"

"Then what are you waiting for? Do you want your little friend to die?"

One of the underlings took a large burlap sack off his back and held it out. Something was inside, frantically trying to get free.

"Coco!"

The animal inside the bag meowed in response to its owner's voice. The boys had captured Zwei's cat.

That's so cruel...

Cecilia bit her lower lip. The other underling took out a knife and pointed it at the wiggling sack.

"Hurry up or you'll see some blood."

"N-no, please don't hurt Coco!"

"I don't take orders from devil spawn!"

The boss of the trio kicked Zwei in the stomach when he tried getting closer to the sack, sending his small body flying. The boy slammed into a tree. He groaned quietly and laboriously got back on his feet.

"D-don't hurt her—I've got the money!"

He produced some bills out of his breast pocket. Cecilia was witnessing one rich boy extorting money from another; it was a hefty sum.

The chief bully grabbed the money and pocketed it without hesitation.

"I needed that. My dad cut off my allowance for overspending. Would you believe that?"

"I gave you the money. What more do you want?"

"Hmm, how about that brooch? Give me that, too."

He grabbed Zwei by the collar and pointed to his chest, where a brooch with a large green gemstone glittered. It would probably fetch a high price.

"You're not going to say no to me, are you?"

"I—I can't giv—"

"Shut up and hand it over!"

I can't stand by and do nothing!

Cecilia picked up a broom that was leaning against the wall next to her and ran out of her hiding place. She rushed at the bullies' boss and swung the broom at him without losing momentum, striking him in the solar plexus. He crumpled with a groan. Her sudden attack left his flunkies dumbfounded.

"What the hell?!"

It didn't take long for the one more used to fighting to recover, though. He tried to stab at Cecilia with his knife, but she used Gilbert's Artifact to repel the blade. It clinked as if striking metal, the force of the rebound sending it up into the air. Cecilia caught the dagger and aimed it at the other underling's neck.

"Your game's up. Give him back the money and the cat, and I'll let you go."

"What are you—?"

"Do as I said and get lost!"

She glared at them. The bullies shuddered and exchanged glances.

"W-we're getting out of here!"

"Right!"

The underlings lifted their boss up by his arms and turned tail. Cecilia relaxed the tension in her back and touched the Artifact to release its protective spell.

This isn't how I imagined my first meeting with Zwei playing out...

She could've just stayed hidden until the end, but it simply wouldn't be in her character.

At least I didn't make a bad impression on him, so I guess this works just fine.

She glanced at Zwei, who was staring wide-eyed in astonishment.

"Are you all right?"

"Er, yes, I am. Thank you... Oh, Coco!"

Zwei hurried over to the bouncing sack and untied it. A familiar-looking kitten jumped out.

"Wait, I know you..."

Cecilia had seen this cat before. Back before the start of the Selection Ceremony, she'd run away from the Prince Cecil Fan Club into the school courtyard and come across this very same kitten, injured at the time. She'd wrapped her handkerchief around its wounded paw, which through an unfortunate chain of events led to Oscar's insistence that Cecil set up an encounter with Cecilia for him.

"I see, so your name's Coco!"

As if in answer, the kitten meowed adorably.

"You know my cat?"

"Uh-huh. We've met once before."

"Really?"

Zwei blinked, surprised. Cecilia suddenly had a eureka moment.

Wait, isn't this my chance to raise his affection? We're off to a good start, so now I just have to keep this conversation going!

She imagined their chat going in exactly the direction she wanted it.

> **Cecilia:** *"Your cat is so adorable!"*
> **Zwei:** *"Isn't she? She's the cutest!"*
> **Cecilia:** *"Yes, she is! I love her!"*
> **Zwei:** *"You seem like someone I could get along with. Let's be friends!"*
> **Cecilia:** *"Sure! I was just about to suggest that myself!"*

Perfect!

She did a little fist pump. Now she'd only need Zwei to introduce her to his brother so she could befriend him, too.

The goal is to get their friendship levels to where we can have lunch together!

That was the objective she'd set for herself. While she couldn't be sure that would be enough to trigger the True Love route, it would definitely count as having established a friendship. Cecilia smiled at Zwei.

"By the way, your cat is—"

"Eeek!"

Zwei shuddered and fell down on his rear when she turned toward him. Cecilia followed his gaze to see what had frightened him and saw that it was fixed on the knife, which she was still holding in her hand. She had accidentally pointed it at him.

"Oh, sorry!"

Just as she panicked and was going to chuck the knife away...

"Zwei!"

A moment after she heard that ear-splitting cry, a rock hit the back of her hand. The sudden pain and surprise made her drop the knife.

"Oww!"

Then she felt a jolt of pain in her shoulder.

"Argh!"

It was only after she fell onto her back that she understood she'd been kicked. Staring down from above was a face identical to Zwei's, save for the fact that his fringe and braid were on the opposite side of his head, like a mirror image.

"Huh? E-Eins?"

"What have you done to Zwei?!"

Cecilia stiffened at this unexpected accusation. She tried to picture how what she was doing might have seemed to an observer.

Er... It seem like Eins misunderstood the situation?

If Eins only saw his brother on the ground and her pointing a knife at him, he must have thought she was threatening him. Like those three bullies who had run away... To make matters worse, the money she'd made them return to Zwei was still lying at her feet—seeming like incriminating evidence.

"How to explain..."

Beads of sweat formed on her forehead. Since she looked like the aggressor, Eins wouldn't trust anything she said in her defense. It would just sound like she was making excuses. Still, she needed to clear up this mix-up somehow. Before she could think of a way out of this, however, Zwei got to his feet and rushed to his brother's side.

"E-Eins, it's not what you think—"

"And you, Zwei. What are you doing, letting this scrawny brat intimidate you?! And what did I tell you about calling me right away if anyone messes with you?!"

Eins was so worked up that he wouldn't listen to anything Zwei was trying to say. He unceremoniously grabbed his brother by the arm, picked up the money, and shoved it into his pocket. Then he turned his back on Cecilia.

"Try it again and I'll make you regret it!"

"I—I won't..."

"Zwei, we're going! You too, Coco!"

Hearing its name, the cat meowed cheerfully. The two boys and their feline companion walked off as Cecilia lay in the dirt. She sighed, gazing at the clouds drifting above.

"Why did it have to end up like this?"

The shoulder Eins had kicked really hurt.

"I'm going to destroy them. I'll crush House Machias," growled Gilbert.

About half an hour had passed since Cecilia's unfortunate encounter with the twins. She and Gilbert had locked themselves in an empty classroom. He was tending to the wound on the back of her hand. She smiled wryly.

"Eins simply mistook me for a bully. Don't get so mad at him..."

"How can I not get mad when he had the gall to not only throw a rock at you, but also kick you for no reason? And he wouldn't let Zwei explain anything."

"Well, yeah."

"See, you can't excuse his behavior. He's making a mistake if he thinks he can get away with abusing a duke's daughter like that!"

"He doesn't know I'm a duke's daughter, Gil!"

His icy tone scared her. On the one hand, it was nice that he'd gotten so angry on her behalf, but on the other, Eins really had just been trying to protect his brother. He didn't deserve her brother's vilification.

Gilbert took out a cotton swab soaked in alcohol for disinfecting wounds from the first aid kit and pressed it to Cecilia's hand. She squirmed.

"Ow, ow, ow! Be gentler, Gil!"

"I am."

"But it stings! Ow!"

The wound didn't bother her so much, but the rubbing alcohol burned. Noticing that her eyes were filling up with tears, Gilbert grew concerned.

"You know, I think we should have Dr. Mordred take a look at it. I'm sure he can get it sorted out in no time."

"I thought about it, but I wouldn't want him to notice the bruise on my shoulder…"

It was too close to her Holy Maiden mark. If Dr. Mordred saw that her shoulder was hurting and asked her to show him the bruise, he might also stumble upon the mark. He didn't even know that Cecil was really a girl yet.

"Speaking of your shoulder, is it okay? Can you raise your arm?"

"I can…up to here."

She only managed to bring it halfway up, and she couldn't straighten it to the side, either. Gilbert's face clouded.

"Does it hurt if you move it more?"

"Yeah. He nailed me right in the joint. Um, but it's not like I can't lift my arm at all, so I'm sure it'll be fine!"

Cecilia did her best to sound cheerful. She didn't want to worry Gilbert, so she smiled through the pain and struck a cool pose. Her brother sighed.

"I get that you think it's no big deal, but let me have a look."

"Wait, why?"

"I want to make sure you don't have broken bones. Plus, something tells me that you're making a brave face to put me at ease."

"Ha-ha…"

She tittered, embarrassed that he'd seen right through her. Gilbert drew closer.

"Let me see it."

"But..."

"Why not? Unless you're hiding something?"

His slender fingers reached for the buttons at her collar. He unfastened the first one without a hint of hesitation and Cecilia tensed up.

"Eek!"

Suddenly, her face grew hot, followed by her entire body. She could scarcely endure the gentle touch of his fingertips brushing against her skin as he undid the buttons.

He's doing this out of concern for me, so I can't push him away... But...

She couldn't decide how to react. Never before had a man attempted to undress her, not even in her past life. Cecilia hadn't realized how mature Gilbert had grown until this moment; now the touch of his hands and the proximity of his body was sending her heart racing.

He's not taking off all my clothes. There's no reason to panic!

But people don't stop fretting just because they've told themselves it was unreasonable.

Completely unfazed, Gilbert undid three of her buttons and pulled down the sleeve to get a look at her shoulder. He examined it with dismay.

"It's swollen, just as I thought. Hmm, but I suppose it'll heal on its own. Let me know if it gets any worse, though... Wait, your face is flushed? Are you running a fever?"

"N-no, I'm not... It's just that...this situation's a bit embarrassing, you know?"

She said this without looking at him, but she could tell that her statement had made him freeze up. His fingertips quivered as he uttered a small "Oh..." He must have been so concerned about her physical well-being that it hadn't occurred to him that he was making her uncomfortable. He quickly released his grip on her clothes.

"I'm sorry…"

"Don't worry about it…"

Cecilia buttoned up her shirt, blushing, while Gilbert just stood there. At that moment, she really hated herself.

Why did I have to blush in the first place?!

He hadn't meant anything untoward, so why had she reacted like that? That only made things more awkward for him. Now she was certain she'd put him off. She had those memories from her past life, of romancing him in the game, but he didn't. He saw Cecilia as nothing more than a sister, and sisters didn't blush at their brother's touch.

Cecilia slapped her cheeks, trying to get herself together. The snappy sound seemed to do the trick. She glanced up to see Gilbert staring at her, his lips in an upward arch.

"Are you…pleased about something?"

"Yeah."

"And what is it?"

"You blushed at me, right?"

She didn't understand. Why would that make him happy? She looked at him sideways, wondering if this was some kind of joke, but Gilbert changed the topic.

"So, do you think you'll become friends?"

"What?"

"With the twins. You've got to befriend them, right?"

Her earlier embarrassment forgotten, she drew close to Gilbert again.

"Ah, yeah! I actually came up with a plan. But I'll need you to lend me a hand."

"Sure."

His unconditional helpfulness returned a smile to her face.

Three days later…

"I'm going to make custard!"

In lieu of her school uniform, Cecilia was wearing an apron and a chef head wrap. One of her hands was on her hip, while in the other, she held a kitchen spatula—not that this last utensil was even needed for making a custard.

Gilbert, Lean, and Cecilia were in the dorm's communal kitchen. Anyone could use it after booking a slot, but the high-born students had little interest in doing their own cooking, so the kitchen and its contents were pristine.

Both Gilbert and Lean were unenthusiastic, to say the least. Cecilia's brother spoke up.

"I'm sorry, but I'm not sure I follow."

"Oh, come on, it's simple! I'll make custard to give to Eins and Zwei!"

That evidently didn't clear anything up for Gilbert, who stared at her with his brow furrowed. Cecilia pointed at him with her index finger.

"You see, there are a few different ways you can raise affection of love interests in dating sims, but the main two are selecting the right dialogue choices and giving them presents they like!"

"So Eins and Zwei like custard, and that's why you're going to make it for them?"

"Yes, exactly! I already got the recipe from the dorm chef! I even got all the ingredients, in exchange for helping carry some stuff to the pantry!"

Cecilia was so pleased with how she'd gotten everything organized that she puffed out her chest.

"You have a very good memory, remembering that the twins liked custard," remarked Lean.

In the game, you can go to the Personal Info section of the menu to check facts about the love interests, such as their height, weight, favorite color, dislikes—all sorts of detailed information. That said,

Cecilia had never looked around there much. And besides, why would she even look at the Personal Info page for the twins when she had never completed their routes?

Cecilia pointed to a notepad on a table behind them.

"This is where I got the info from!"

"What's that?"

"Grace's notes on the twins' route!"

"Huh?"

Though Cecilia was chirpy, her brother had a wary look on his face.

"When did you get that?"

"Hmm, the day after the tea party? I asked Grace for hints, so she wrote all that down for me!"

"I keep telling you to share things like that with me..."

No matter how many times Gilbert asked her to keep him in the loop, she always somehow forgot. As Cecilia leafed through the notes, she noticed out of the corner of her eye him put his head in his hands and heave a sigh.

"Oh, but you know, it's just general info about them. Their likes and dislikes, that sort of thing!"

"Really? Why isn't there more?"

"Well, you see..."

Cecilia put a finger on her chin and explained what Grace told her when giving her the notes.

"I wrote down their general info and added some remarks about what to watch out for when completing their routes, but I cannot give you any more information about House Machias beyond that."

"Why not? You don't remember?"

"There is the fact that my memories of the twins' route are no longer crystal clear, yes. But the main reason is that it would weigh on my conscience to divulge their secrets without their permission..."

Grace seemed uneasy, like she was torn between her willingness to help Cecilia and her sense of what was morally right to do.

That explanation didn't satisfy Gilbert.

"And you just thanked her, took the notebook, and went on your way? Even though your life depends on getting that intel?"

"Yup! It wouldn't be fair to the Machias twins if somebody was telling their deepest secrets to others just because they asked, don't you think?"

"Well, yeah, but…"

While he could understand Grace's reasoning, he didn't accept it. If he were in Cecilia's place, he'd have insisted on getting the whole story out of Grace, ethics be damned.

Lean crossed her arms and gave Cecilia a stern look.

"Gift-giving is a good way of raising the target's affection, but let me ask you this: When did you learn to cook?"

"Huh?"

"In your past life, your home economics group failed a cooking exam because of your ineptitude. I seriously doubt you're capable of making something as delicate as custard."

After that disaster in the kitchen, Cecilia became the designated salad tosser for the rest of the year.

"I'm sure I can do it! The chef said it's really easy!"

"The level of difficulty doesn't mean anything when you have exactly zero cooking ability to begin with."

"Don't worry! This recipe is foolproof!"

"I was right, wasn't I? You never learned how to make food!"

Lean wouldn't be placated. Gilbert suddenly turned and headed for the door, but Lean prevented him from leaving.

"Where are you going, Gilbert? You're not running away, are you?"

"No, but I thought I should go and get some indigestion medicine just in case."

"Forget about that and talk Cecilia out of this ridiculous plan!"

"Why me?"

"Because she's your sister!"

Gilbert paused and thought about it for a moment.

"I would stop her if she was doing something that might put her life in danger."

"That's not being supportive. You're enabling her to do the stupidest things!" Lean screamed, getting worked up. She just wasn't going to let it go.

"And even IF the custard you made turned out okay by some strange coincidence, the twins might not think it's anything special. They're aristocrats, raised on the most exquisite cuisine. If you serve them custard that's just 'all right,' they might even get offended!"

"I've thought about this, too, and I've planned accordingly!"

"Really?"

Lean didn't seem convinced in the slightest.

"I'll hold a tasting session before giving the custard to the twins!"

"Tasting session?"

Just as Lean repeated that in a quivering voice, the door to the kitchen opened to reveal a familiar crew.

"Is this the right place?"

"Gotta be! Cecil's going to treat us to something yummy! I can't wait!"

Huey and Jade came in first.

"But... Why is the tasting session in the kitchen? I'm not sure I like this."

"Let's just go inside and see what's going on. Maybe that's where Cecil ordered the food to be delivered."

Next entered Dante and Oscar.

"Thank you all for coming!"

Cecilia greeted them with a big smile.

"I'm going to try my hand at making custard!"

Dante, with his extraordinarily keen ability to sense danger, spun on his heel immediately.

"I'm going to try my hand at making custard!"

The first thing Oscar thought when he heard that was, *this had better be a joke.* Cecil had already proved himself to be a klutz during the field trip, and he was well aware of his inability to cook. It was quite incredible that he'd now offer to whip something up for all of them.

The prince snapped out of his reverie when Dante, who was next to him, sprung for the door. Oscar grabbed him by the arm to stop him from leaving. The other boy smiled foolishly, without a hint of guilt.

"Where were you going?"

"I just remembered I've gotta do something!"

That was a lie. Before they headed to the kitchen, Dante had cheerfully told Oscar that he was glad for the distraction since he had nothing better to do.

Oscar stared him down accusingly. Dante whispered quietly, so that Cecil wouldn't hear.

"I love Cecil, he's great. But his cooking skills are…"

He made a zero with his thumb and index finger.

"So I'm out of here. Bye!"

"No, wait!"

But Dante quickly wriggled out from Oscar's grip and bolted through the door.

Lean was the next to bail. When the boys came in, she headed over to Huey, her boyfriend, and took his hand. Then she flashed him a charming, bashful grin.

"Lord Huey, how lovely that you came here to get me! I'm so happy to see you!"

"Came to get you?" Huey replied, confused. Lean ignored him and instead turned to the others.

"Lord Huey and I are going on a date! It's such a pity that we won't get to try Lord Cecil's custard, but we can't cancel our plans. That means more for the rest of you, though! Please do let me know your impressions, so that I may enjoy it vicariously through you!"

She led Huey out of the kitchen, giving superficial niceties throughout their improvised retreat. The group had dwindled to only four people: Gilbert, who had a soft spot for his sister, her fiancé Oscar, the unsuspecting Jade, and the starry-eyed trouble-maker (?) Cecilia.

"But why are you making custard out of the blue?"

When Oscar asked her that, Cecilia was already getting started. The counter where she was measuring out the sugar and milk was a mess. She raised her head at his question.

"Um, I want to give some to the Machias brothers as an apology after I upset them."

"An apology? I see…"

Although Oscar didn't pursue it further, he suspected there was more to it than Cecilia was letting on. After all, she had been so eager to find the Machiases at the tea party. It probably had something to do with the reason why she was pretending to be a boy, so he decided to avoid prying any further.

Meanwhile, Cecilia had finished preparing the ingredients and was standing in front of the mixing bowl, notes from the dorm's chef in hand.

"Okay! The first thing to go in is…my secret ingredient! Red hot chili peppers!"

"What? No!"

Nothing else that day had given Oscar a reason to raise his voice as high as Cecilia's bizarre addition to the custard. She shot him a questioning look, clueless as to why he'd stopped her. Her innocently naive expression was adorable, but Oscar couldn't let it distract him.

"Why would you put chili in it?! You definitely *don't* want that in a custard!"

"You don't know this simple trick, then, huh? Adding a touch of heat to a sweet dish emphasizes the sweetness!"

She said it as confidently as if she were talking about adding a pinch of salt to a watermelon. But everyone knows it's salt that's supposed to bring out the sweetness, not spice. To make matters worse, it wasn't a few bits of finely chopped chili that she wanted to put in or even a few slices of it, no—she had WHOLE chilies in her hand.

Before Oscar could think of how to explain to her why those spices had no place in a custard in a way she would understand, Cecilia threw them into the bowl without hesitation. Oscar reckoned there were about a dozen or so. It was only the first step of her cooking adventure, but what she was making had already lost the right to be called a custard. It was now some experimental dish.

As Oscar stared completely dazed by what he'd just witnessed, Cecilia moved on to the next ingredient.

"And now the eggs! Smash!"

She cracked them against the edge of the bowl with brute force. This wasn't a mistake, no—she really went for it. The yolks splattered all over the bowl but that wasn't the worst part. Bits of eggshell fell in as well. It was going to be a pain in the neck to fish them all out.

"Oops, I got some shell pieces in there also… Oh well! It's bonus calcium!"

"You can't be serious—"

"I guess I'll have to crush them, though. A custard isn't supposed to have crunchy bits…"

She proceeded to crush the biggest piece of shell with the spatula she had been wielding earlier, pressing down with it as if mashing potatoes to break it into ever smaller pieces.

"Okay, that'll do it!"

Oscar wondered for a moment if he was hallucinating. At this point, he'd given up on trying to correct Cecilia's misconceptions about cooking and had resigned himself to bearing witness to the culinary crimes she was committing. He glanced over at Gilbert, who was also watching impassively. Then he sidled closer and whispered:

"Is it always like this?"

"Yes. Unfortunately, Cecil likes cooking and always rejects any help offered...," Gilbert replied pitifully, but with a faint smile. Oscar understood that the other boy's silence was due to his stoic acceptance of the fact that nothing he could say would prevent this disaster from unfolding before their very eyes.

Cecilia was now getting ready to add another ingredient. She lugged over a jug so large she had to hold it with both hands. It was full of fine white crystals.

"Next, sugar!"

"Hold on! Are you sure that's not salt?!"

"Yup, I checked beforehand! I wouldn't make a beginner's mistake like that, you know! Okay, here it goes!"

Instead of using a spoon, she tipped the jug over the bowl, pouring in a ridiculous amount of sugar.

"Oops, I added a bit too much."

The sugar was piled high in the bowl like a little snowy mountain. Cecilia serenely picked up the spatula again and used it to haphazardly stir the contents of the bowl.

"The sweeter the better, right?"

The crunching noise coming from the bowl didn't sound like what you should hear when making custard. Oscar's face froze in terror.

"Don't worry. It's not enough to kill a person."

"So are you telling me it's fine as long as it doesn't kill us?!"

"Well, it's not like we can do anything about it. Cecil won't listen."

Oscar didn't know what to say to Gilbert, who'd made peace with his fate. He felt a tug at his sleeve and glanced down to see Jade clutching it, tears welling up in his eyes.

"It's getting a bit scary. Is he going to feed that to us? Do we have to eat it?!"

"Well…"

"I…I will stop him!"

Catching on to the danger they were in, Jade took it upon himself to save them from Cecil's cooking. Just as he was about to say something, however, Cecilia turned to face the boys and gave them a blindingly bright smile.

"Thanks for doing this for me, guys! I'm a total amateur at this. I've never really made food for anyone outside of my family before, so it's going to be *so* helpful to have your feedback!"

His sincere gratitude, coupled with that heart-melting smile, made Jade swallow his words of protest.

It's too late to try to worm my way out of this…

The three boys stood silently, waiting for Cecilia to finish cooking her approximation of a custard.

An hour later, Cecilia's three victims were barely showing signs of life. Oscar was slumped in a chair, like a knocked-out boxer. Gilbert stood covering his mouth with his hand, perhaps worried that if he tried sitting down, he might not get back up again. Jade was sprawled out on his back over three chairs lined up together, his eyes open but unseeing. Only their poisoner was still in good shape, though she was anxiously hovering beside the boys.

"I-I'm so sorry! I was sure it would be delicious!"

She was nearly in tears. Oscar raised his head.

"How you could have possibly expected it to pass for food is beyond me."

"It could've been worse. At least all of the ingredients were edible this time."

"My mouth's burning... I feel as if I've been eating grit..."

Yet somehow, they'd all managed to clean their plates. Only Cecilia's slice of the custard-like object remained.

Jade got up shakily and latched onto Gilbert.

"Gil, help..."

"What's wrong?"

"I'm gonna hurl..."

"Huh?!"

"I can't walk alone... Take me to the restroom... Urgh...!"

Jade shuddered, then doubled over to retch. He was clearly at his limit.

"All right, all right! Just try to hold it in until I get you there!"

Gilbert put his arm around Jade's shoulders and led him to the door, but before they left, he turned back to glare at Oscar.

"We won't be gone long!"

He was warning the prince not to try anything funny. Just in case.

Since Oscar had figured out that Cecil was really Cecilia, Gilbert was being even more vigilant in keeping him away from her. Oscar used to think her brother was just very devoted to his sister, but he'd started to suspect of late that his overprotectiveness of her wasn't entirely wholesome.

Having said his piece, Gilbert left with Jade. Cecilia had been apologizing in a tearful voice until they disappeared down the corridor. She really seemed shattered. Not only was her custard a total failure, but she'd also made Jade very sick. Cecilia hung her head in despair.

"Don't let it get to you so much. We all make mistakes sometimes," Oscar told her.

"I guess so..."

While Oscar wasn't quite sure that this disaster could be written off as "just a mistake," he wanted to say anything to make her feel better. Seeing that his comment didn't help, he sighed and stood up. Next, he undid the buttons at his cuffs and rolled up his sleeves.

"All right, let's get cleaning!"

"What?" Cecilia gazed up at him, her eyes moist with tears.

"Doing something productive will help both of us feel better."

He reached for the mixing bowl, but Cecilia hurried to stop him.

"You don't need to do anything, Oscar! I'll tidy up!"

"I'd rather not leave it to you, or it may end as badly as your cooking."

"Oh... Um..."

She shrank back again. Oscar smiled at her.

"I was only teasing you. Let me help, since I have nothing else to do anyway."

"Right... Okay, let's do it together."

They started washing tableware and kitchen utensils in the sink, standing side by side. Cecilia pouted as she scrubbed burnt sugar from the saucepan.

"But where did I go wrong with my custard?"

"Don't try to make another one before you figure that out. You'd only waste ingredients."

"Well, yeah, but..."

"If you're so intent on giving a custard to the Machias twins, either buy one or have someone help you make it. Otherwise, you'd better start planning your elaborate apology for giving them food poisoning."

"I suppose you're right..."

Cecilia smiled self-deprecatingly at his not unreasonable advice and nodded gravely.

"By the way, are you feeling okay? You ate all of your serving."

"I'm fine for now. It will probably hit me by the evening."

"You shouldn't have finished it..."

"I couldn't have left it uneaten. You made it."

Oscar shook off water from the spatula and the mixing bowl

and set them on a kitchen towel to dry them. Only then did he notice that Cecilia was staring at him. She smiled bashfully when their eyes met.

"You're such a good friend. Thanks."

She went back to scrubbing the saucepan, but her spirits seemed to have lifted a bit. Oscar peered down at the top of her head as she was hunched over the sink.

"I wouldn't have done it for just a friend."

Very slowly, Cecilia raised her head and met his gaze again.

"I'd only ever do that for you."

It took about three seconds for her face to turn bright red. For once, his implied meaning didn't go over her head. She quickly glanced away, stammering "R-really?" in an oddly high-pitched voice.

For a few minutes, neither of them said a word. The only sounds were clanks and chinks of tableware being cleaned and put away, which somehow unnerved Oscar. Cecilia, still blushing, spoke up at last.

"You like me, Oscar?"

"Yeah."

"In the, um, romantic sense?"

"That's right."

Cecilia had needed to muster all her willpower to get that question out, but Oscar readily answered without beating around the bush. Maybe he should have elaborated on it somewhat, but he couldn't think of anything else to add. He glanced at Cecilia out of the corner of his eye. She didn't seem put off by what he'd said, just confused. Her eyes were wide open, darting every which way.

"Oscar, I've got to tell you something..."

"Hmm?"

"I'm not actually a— Yikes!"

When she turned to him, she gestured with her hand, forgetting about the open tap. The high-pressure stream of water hit the back of her hand and splashed onto her face. It also got on Oscar.

"Cecil…"

"I'm sorry…"

It had taken only a moment for the two of them to get doused. Cecilia's entire outfit was sopping wet, while Oscar only got caught on the left side.

"Seriously, what were you thinking…? Huh?"

As he unconsciously dropped his gaze from her face to her chest, he noticed something showing through her wet shirt—a red rose mark.

I know what that is…

It was the symbol signifying that she was one of the Holy Maiden candidates.

He stared, transfixed, but then something else below the mark drew his eye. Through the semitransparent fabric of her wet shirt, he could clearly make out her cleavage, conspicuous despite her best attempts to flatten her chest by binding it tightly. In fact, her breasts couldn't be contained by the strip of fabric she'd wrapped around them and were now peeking out over the top…

"Are you all right, Oscar?"

"Y-yes, I am! D-don't come any closer!"

He backed away from Cecilia, who took a step toward him. Her wet shirt was also clinging to her midriff, exposing her curves and alabaster skin. Nevertheless, she still hadn't noticed anything herself.

I—I suppose I should tell her? No, I can't! She's trying to hide the fact that she's a girl from me…

If he told her that her shirt had turned see-through, she would realize that he'd literally seen through her disguise. What if she had to flee to another country because of this and he'd never see her again? He didn't want that. It would be unbearable.

"What's wrong, Oscar?"

What should I do...?

He turned his face away, unable to look at her in this state. If only she'd kept the apron on!

All of a sudden, he heard voices in the corridor. A group of boys was approaching the kitchen.

Oh no... They can't see her like this!

The high-born students who frequented the academy generally didn't use the kitchens. They were accustomed to having other people cook for them. But there were also other students here with a background like Jade, commoners whose families had only recently come into money. They would occasionally go to the kitchens to prepare simple meals or brew tea. What if the approaching group was about to do that?

The rose mark would be a dead giveaway that Cecil was a girl and a sought-after Holy Maiden at that!

Besides, I don't want anyone else to see my fiancée looking like this!

He took off his jacket and put it over her shoulders, trying to close it over her chest to hide it from view. Cecilia resisted, completely oblivious of her appearance.

"No, take it back, Oscar! It'll only get wet!"

"Don't worry about that!"

"I can't help worrying! I don't want it!"

The footsteps outside were drawing nearer. Cecilia was trying to take the jacket off. And Oscar was so distraught that he couldn't think straight.

These three factors conspired to make him choose an untypically daring solution.

"Just cover yourself!"

He pulled Cecilia into a tight embrace, so that she wouldn't be able to take the jacket off, pressing her against his body.

This should do it...

"O-O-Oscar?!"

"Stay still!"

The door to the kitchen opened, and someone walked in. Seeing who it was had a sobering effect on Oscar.

"Oh."

"What the…?"

It was Gilbert. Jade wasn't with him—perhaps Gilbert had left him back at the infirmary. A group of chatting students walked past the kitchen.

"Your Highness, what is the meaning of this?" Gilbert growled after shutting the door. Never before had he glared at Oscar with so much contempt. The prince's expression went rigid.

"It's not what you're thinking…"

"Really? How about you release Cecil first, before making excuses!"

Gilbert's lips stretched into a smile so terrifying he looked truly demonic.

The day after her unplanned near-poisoning of the country's crown prince, Cecilia was sitting on a bench in the courtyard, gazing up at the sky. She sighed.

"I don't know what to do now…"

Her custard idea had ended in complete failure, both literally and figuratively leaving a bad taste in the mouths of the friends she'd roped in as tasters, and now she was without a plan. She hadn't seen the twins since the tea party, and she was sure that her affection level with them was zero at best.

"And on top of that, I got Oscar's clothes soaked and made Gilbert mad… It couldn't have gone worse!"

She straightened her arms and legs and did a big stretch. There was the matter of what Oscar had said, too, but her head was already almost bursting from everything that happened recently, so she decided not to think about him for the time being. This wasn't something she could resolve on her own, anyway, with how complicated the situation and their relationship was.

Feeling something soft rub against her legs, Cecilia looked down to find a familiar kitten at her feet.

"Hi, Coco."

"Coco!"

Someone else was calling the cat. She turned to see who it was...

"Zwei?"

"Oh... It's you..."

It was one of the Machias twins. His braid was on the left side, which was how she knew it was Zwei. When their eyes met, he made a sad face and hung his head.

"I'm so sorry about what happened the other day! I couldn't get Eins to understand that you helped me out. Did he... Did he hurt you?"

He looked as if he might burst into tears. Cecilia made a circle with her arm, on the side where Eins had kicked her in the shoulder.

"Nah, he didn't! I'm fine!"

"Thank goodness..."

He put a hand to his chest, visibly relieved. Truth be told, when Cecilia moved her arm, she'd flinched for a moment as a sharp spasm of pain ran through her shoulder, but she managed to smile through it.

She scooted over to one side of the bench, making space for Zwei. He seemed baffled by this at first, but he didn't hesitate long before sitting down next to her. Coco jumped up onto his lap and curled up comfortably for a nap.

Stroking the sleepy kitty, Zwei bowed his head and apologized to Cecilia again.

"I really am so sorry. I've been encouraging my brother to

apologize to you, but everything I say goes in one ear and out the other. It can be extremely difficult to change his mind once he gets an idea stuck in his head..."

Zwei told her that he'd tried to explain to Eins that it was all a mix-up, but it only made his brother more suspicious. He was now convinced that Cecilia had threatened Zwei and forced him to say those things.

"I can totally see how he misunderstood my intentions! It really looked like I was the baddie! But don't worry, it doesn't bother me one bit!"

"It's very magnanimous of you to say that. You're such a good person, Cecil."

Still looking down at the ground, Zwei smiled gently. He was so cute and pretty you could mistake him for a girl. No wonder he was a love interest in the game.

Huh... Wait a second... This is actually going in the right direction!

Since this encounter was entirely unexpected, it took a moment before Cecilia assessed what was going on and noticed that it was a great opportunity for her to raise Zwei's affection level. First, she'd get it higher through a pleasant conversation and then have him introduce her to his brother, so that she could raise his fondness for her as well! Yes, this was the way to do it!

But what should I talk about with him? His cat? Or...

There was something else that had been nagging at her. She shifted on the bench to face him.

"Tell me, does that sort of stuff happen to you often?"

"What sort of stuff?"

"You know... Getting bullied?"

Thinking back to that scene, her impression was that it hadn't been the first time those boys tried to extort money from Zwei. Both sides had seemed to know the drill. Maybe it wasn't happening daily, but it must have been a regular occurrence.

Zwei opened his eyes wide and then nodded gravely.

"Yes. It wasn't every day, but it did happen often, yes."

"Why do they bully you?"

"Because I'm a twin."

He replied so quietly it was almost a whisper, staring down at his shoes. Cecilia was mystified by this.

"Huh? What's that got to do with anything?"

"You don't know?"

"No?"

She really had no clue. Zwei seemed perplexed by this. When he spoke, it was in a voice so faint she had to strain her ears to hear him.

"Since ancient times, identical twins have been reviled as devil spawn."

"What?"

"There's a belief that the demons the goddess banished were all identical twins. It's especially strong among people from the north, where the temple is."

The three bullies were from this region, and they were picking on both Eins and Zwei because they saw them as "devil spawn."

"You can't be serious! They're mean to you just because you're twins?!"

"It's not that shocking. Our birth caused an uproar in our homeland. People were demanding that my family kill at least one of us."

Cecilia was at a loss for words. It shocked her to learn that there was such strong superstition in this world, and it chilled her to the bone that some people thought it would please their goddess to kill innocent babies.

"Eins is fierce, so he fights back whenever he gets picked on. But I'm not like him… It's always been him coming to my rescue."

That's what Eins had thought Cecilia was doing when he came upon her accidentally pointing a knife at Zwei. It was a familiar scene

63

to him, so he did what he usually did: attack the person he thought was the bully.

Cecilia got up abruptly, having thought of something. She turned to Zwei.

"Let's go!"

"Huh?"

"To talk to those bullies! It's crazy what they're doing!"

She was ready for action. Zwei stood, frightened by her sudden proposition.

"N-no, wait!"

"Don't you worry about a thing! I can recognize them. If they won't listen to my words, we'll reach an understanding through fisticuffs!"

Cecilia Sylvie was nothing if not impulsive. To her credit, despite the fact she was ready for violence, she was aiming for discourse rather than coercion.

But her heroic proclamation only made Zwei more panicked.

"Y-you don't need to do that!"

"If it gets scary, you can always hide!"

"No, I mean it, you don't need to talk to them!"

"It'll be fine. Don't worry about me!"

"What I'm trying to say is, it's all right now."

"Huh?"

It finally dawned on Cecilia that Zwei, desperately holding her back by her sleeve, wasn't refusing her help because he was feeling too shy. She let her raised fists drop. Reassured, Zwei plopped back down onto the bench and slowly exhaled.

"They stopped bullying me recently."

"What, really?"

"Apparently, their parents received letters of complaint from House Sylvie."

"Did you say House Sylvie?"

Cecilia certainly hadn't been expecting her family name to come up.

"Yes. The duke and duchess wrote that my brother and I are friends of his son and that they will not tolerate bullying. At least that's what I heard. It's strange, though, because as far as I know, neither Eins nor I are friends with anyone from House Sylvie."

He gave a flustered smile, but there was relief in his eyes, too.

Is Gil behind this?

It was well within the realm of possibility that Gilbert asked their parents to write those letters after Cecilia got involved with the Machiases. He'd been furious when she got hurt, so he probably wouldn't hesitate to ask their parents a favor like that if it was to keep Cecilia safe.

"But even without those kids bothering us, nobody talks to me and my brother. I bet they've intimidated the other students by telling them to steer clear of us. This is our only friend."

He stroked Coco's soft fur. Cecilia wasn't sure whether the cat lived at the academy or if Zwei had brought him from his home, but in any case, they seemed to be attached to each other.

She went round to stand in front of Zwei.

"Do you want to be friends with me?"

Zwei's emerald eyes grew as huge as saucers.

"What do you say? I'd really like to be friends with you! Oh, and your brother, too, of course!"

"You want to be friends with Eins, too?"

She nodded resolutely. Zwei darted his eyes around as he considered it. Had her abrupt offer of friendship made him wary?

Cecilia crouched in front of him and looked up at his face.

"Um… Would you please be my friend?"

"…Okay."

After a moment of hesitation, he took the hand she'd offered him. Cecilia immediately broke out into a smile.

"Phew! I was worried you'd say no! Thank you, Zwei!"

"The pleasure's mine…"

Zwei let her shake his hand energetically, looking a bit unsure as to how to respond.

"There's no need to be so formal! We're friends now, so you can act casual with me!"

"Oh, okay."

Just as he nodded, the large bell at the top of the schoolhouse chimed the hour. Cecilia looked up, gasping.

"Shoot! I'm supposed to be meeting up with Lean right now. I'll see you later, Zwei! Let's have lunch together sometime soon!"

"Okay… See you later."

Cecilia heard him give an awkward chuckle as she sped away to meet Lean in one of the classrooms.

Zwei sighed, following Cecilia with his gaze. He blinked, and his eyes took on a sharpness that hadn't been there before. He undid the braid on the left side of his head, combed his hair with his fingers, and redid it on the right side.

He leaned back on the bench exuding an irreverent attitude—unthinkable only moments before—and crossed his legs. Coco jumped down from his lap.

"Hmph. He's just a naive rich boy."

Zwei, or rather Eins, who had been posing as his twin brother, sneered as he kept his eyes fixed in the direction Cecilia had run off.

That morning, Lean announced she was going to collect her dues.

"It's time you repaid me for my assistance at the tea party. Meet me in the usual classroom after school."

* * *

Cecilia was sitting down at a desk in the place they'd agreed to meet, holding a pamphlet. The title on its white cover was *The Legend of Prosper Kingdom: The Ashen Night and Bright Dawn – New Translation.*

"So... What am I looking at?"

"The script."

"What script?"

Cecilia leafed through the pages and saw that they were filled with character names and lines of dialogue. Lean slammed her hands on the table, leaning toward her confused friend, and grinned.

"You're going to star in a play."

"Huh? A play?"

"You heard that right. A play! ♡"

"Hold on a moment!"

Cecilia could HEAR that heart mark in Lean's sugary intonation, and to her, it was a clear warning sign.

"What sort of play do you mean? You're not turning that BL story into a production, are you?!"

"No! I wouldn't mind that, of course, but that's not it this time. Did you even read the title?"

Cecilia checked the cover again.

"It's a legend, see? The contents are totally wholesome this time! I want to stage a completely innocent play based on a local legend!"

That didn't put Cecilia's mind at ease—quite the opposite. This "Legend of Prosper Kingdom" had to be the story about the goddess defeating the demons, right? Which was already what Advent Festival was based on anyway. So what was the point in putting on a play about it? Also, upon second glance, Cecilia noticed that the pamphlet was authored by someone named "Neal"; wasn't that the pen name Lean used when writing BL fiction?

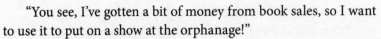

"You see, I've gotten a bit of money from book sales, so I want to use it to put on a show at the orphanage!"

She clapped her hands with glee.

"Advent is just around the corner, so wouldn't a play based on the legend behind it make for an apt opener for that season? I really want to do it for my sisters!"

By "her sisters," Lean must have meant the other girls at Cigogne Orphanage. Now that Cecilia thought about it, there was no way that the kids living there would ever get taken to see a play at a theater since the orphanage was strapped for cash. And even if they could somehow afford a trip, the lords and ladies who frequented those establishments would be very displeased to find out they had to share seats with a throng of shabby orphans.

"I want to invite all the locals and make it a big event! The orphanage has plenty of land, at least, so there's room for a big audience! I still need to think through the logistics of it, but I think we can get a simple stage constructed out of wood outdoors and show it in open air! I'm waiting on a quote to see how much it would cost before deciding on the details!"

She had already requested a quote? Cecilia sighed. Her friend didn't wait around once she set her mind on something.

"But you can't have a play without the actors, and well... I asked Jade what I should do about that, and he offered to introduce me to a troupe of performers who would do it on the cheap. The only problem is that there's a catch..."

"What catch?"

"The leader of the troupe resigned abruptly not long ago, and since they were the main draw, the group hasn't been getting many contracts lately. That's the reason why they've lowered their fees until they recruit another star to replace the one who left. Which is why...I'll need YOU to play the lead!"

"You've got to be kidding! Me as the lead?!"

Cecilia's eyes were practically popping out from shock.

"It's laudable that you want to stage a play for the orphans, and I'm totally behind you on this, but you can't be serious about giving the main role in your production to me!"

"But I don't have anyone else who could do it. The remaining actors in the troupe are kind of lacking in the charisma department."

"Why me, though...?"

"Because charisma is one thing you've got plenty of. I don't know about your acting skills, but all you really need to do is be the Prince Cecil everyone loves!"

And that cinched it. Out of excuses, Cecilia brought a hand to her forehead. To be fair, it did sound like a wholly charitable undertaking. Lean wanted to do something nice for the orphanage where she'd grown up. Cecilia had no reason to object to that; on the contrary, she should be happy to help, but...

Was Lean really telling Cecilia the whole story? Spending all of her hard-earned money on a show for the orphans seemed odd. Lean was pragmatic by nature, so if all she wanted was to reciprocate in some way for the care she received at the orphanage, it would seem more her style to just donate the cash. Did she have an ulterior motive...?

"By the way, you can't say no to this."

"Why?"

Cecilia looked up at her dubiously. Lean flashed her a broad smile and poked the tip of her nose.

"Because that's been our agreement. I told you my help would cost you. You wouldn't break a promise you made to a friend, would you?"

Now Cecilia was sure that Lean had an ulterior motive. Sadly, she'd already sealed her fate. She hung her head, throbbing with a stress-induced headache.

"I won't break our promise..."

"Thank you so very much. Let's try on your costume."

Lean authoritatively took her by the arm and led her to a full-size mirror. Then she held out a costume in front of her, presumably handmade.

"I'm really happy with how this one turned out."

"Wait, you want me to wear THIS?"

"Well, yeah! You'll be the protagonist from the legend!"

Cecilia examined the costume in the mirror. It was a snow-white dress. It looked so immaculate that it almost had an aura of divinity.

"Goddess Cecilia, this is going to be so much fun!"

"Nooooo waaaay!"

Cecilia's scream of shock echoed through the hallway.

When Cecilia finally left the classroom where she met up with Lean, the sun was already setting. Both her shadow and her face were long as she trudged back to the dorm.

"Lean seriously has no consideration for me..."

Cecilia felt utterly dejected thinking back to what her friend had asked of her. She'd begged Lean to give up on the idea, crying that she couldn't possibly appear in a female role in the play, but Lean would not relent.

"It'll be fine, I'll tell everyone you're a boy playing a female character! And anyway, the play will be shown at the orphanage, not a city theater. Students from the academy wouldn't turn up there without reason, and since no one will be announcing your name, the audience won't know who you are! Plus, I have a wig for you to wear on stage. There's no risk in it for you, trust me."

Cecilia did not have faith in Lean's assertion, but her friend was adept at convincing others that everything would turn out fine.

Cecilia looked down at her shoes and stopped.

"I guess it'll be okay..."

Even assuming that Lean wasn't being entirely transparent about her motives, she genuinely wanted to do something for the benefit of the orphanage. In which case, Cecilia could be counted on to help. It was also undeniable that she owed Lean a favor.

She took a deep breath. Just as she was about to start walking again...

"Huh?"

...something dropped down right in front of her nose. There was an ear-piercing noise that sounded like a plate shattering. It was a flowerpot, which had broken upon impact with the ground. Startled, Cecilia looked up and noticed a silhouette of a person—she couldn't tell whether it was a boy or girl—in one of the schoolhouse windows. Noticing her gaze, the stranger quickly vanished back inside.

During lunch break the day after someone had tried to drop a flowerpot on her head, Cecilia went to see Doctor Mordred. It wasn't because she'd gotten hurt.

"Doctor, do you have clear memories of last evening?"

"Excuse me?"

Cecilia had an inkling that it might have been the Killer who'd dropped that flowerpot. Sitting on a stool for patients, she leaned in toward the doctor, who had been eying her quizzically.

"If, by any chance, you have a gap in your memories, please tell me! I promise I won't be angry! I want to help you, too, Doctor!"

"I'm afraid I don't know what you're talking about."

Unaware of the fact that he was the Killer, Mordred sighed, then removed his glasses and rubbed the bridge of his nose. He tended to do that whenever something troublesome came up.

"You come to my office and throw bizarre accusations at me. Whenever it's you, I know I have to brace myself for problems..."

"Well..."

"And what do you mean, you won't get angry at me if I have a gap in my memories? Are you insinuating that me not remembering things causes problems for you?"

Yeah, that's exactly what I'm saying!

She couldn't tell him that, of course. Mordred put his glasses back on, adjusting them with his middle finger. He narrowed his eyes with suspicion from behind his lenses, but Cecilia wouldn't let that put her off.

"A-anyway, where were you last evening?"

"I had dinner with Emily and Grace."

"Between what times?"

"...We met up just before six and were together until about eight."

That would give him an alibi...

Cecilia didn't have a watch, so she didn't know the precise time of the flowerpot incident, but she was sure that it had been after six when she parted ways with Lean.

Does it mean it wasn't the Killer who did that?

But no one besides Dr. Mordred's other personality would have any reason to want to hurt a Holy Maiden candidate at this point, assuming that the Killer hadn't completely disappeared from Mordred's psyche.

"Were you surprised to find out more time had passed than you'd thought at any point in the dinner? Or you were suddenly in a different place than a moment before and you couldn't remember how you got there?"

"No."

"Are you sure?"

"Yes."

That last answer came in a different, higher-pitched voice. Cecilia turned to find Grace, observing her with one eyebrow raised. She'd just entered and was closing the door behind her without looking. She was carrying a man's coat.

"Hello, Grace!"

"And what might you be doing here, Cecil?"

Grace shot her a tired glance. Cecilia stood up to greet her.

"What are YOU doing here, Grace?"

"I came to return this."

She raised the coat to Mordred and handed it to him before giving her thanks.

"Doctor Mordred lent it to me yesterday, since it was a rather chilly evening."

"Ah, really?"

"As I told you, we had dinner together..."

Cecilia wasn't trying to cast doubt on that fact, but she decided to let the matter slide, so she just replied "Right!"

She touched her chin, thinking.

It looks like it really couldn't have been the Killer this time.

Grace confirmed Mordred's alibi. On the one hand, if Mordred had indeed been freed from the Killer, that was terrific. But on the other, it left her guessing as to the identity of the mysterious flower-pot dropper.

"Did something unusual happen?" Grace asked in a whisper, noticing Cecilia's disconcerted expression. Cecilia nodded. The other girl thought for a moment and then took her hand.

"Why don't we go somewhere else for a chat, Cecil?"

"Huh? Um, okay!"

"Wait, where are you going?"

They promptly left the infirmary, ignoring Mordred's pleas.

A few minutes later, Grace and Cecilia were at the back of the schoolhouse. The place seemed rather neglected, and in fact, students rarely hung out there. This was where Cecilia had saved Zwei and Coco from the bullies.

The girls were leaning against the wall.

"...And that made me think the Killer had struck again, so I went to speak with Doctor Mordred."

"I understand what you were doing, but why would you put yourself in harm's way like that?"

"Put myself in harm's way? What do you mean?"

Cecilia widened her eyes at Grace, who frowned in return.

"Haven't you considered what would have happened if Doctor Mordred really still had the remnants of the Killer in him?"

"Oh…"

"And yet you went to see him alone? That would be giving the Killer the perfect opportunity. To strike. Do you have a death wish?"

"Now that you mention it, you're absolutely right…"

She had unconsciously assumed that the Killer was no longer a threat and felt safe going to see Mordred. But if she'd been wrong, that would have changed the situation diametrically. Bringing up the incident from the day before would have been enough for Mordred to switch to the Killer and erase her from existence. He wasn't a character to take lightly.

"At least now you've conclusively proven that there's no trace of the Killer left in Doctor Mordred. I have to say, though, I'm shocked that Gilbert would approve of this foolhardy plan."

"Huh? What's this about Gil?"

"I would have thought that the moment you told him of this, he'd have raised alarm at how ridiculously dangerous it was."

Grace elaborated for the sake of her friend who was always slow on the uptake. She seemed to have gotten the idea that Gilbert was Cecilia's guardian and that Cecilia needed to run everything by him first.

Cecilia scratched her cheek, bemused.

"Actually, I haven't said a word about it to Gil yet."

"What?"

"I didn't want to make him anxious over nothing when I didn't even understand what really happened myself, you know? I was going to tell him after doing a bit of investigating."

Grace's expression grew stony. Now she wasn't just disapproving, but visibly incensed with Cecilia.

"This sort of thinking is what makes people so worried about you."

"But Gil's been busy lately, so I didn't want to bother him…"

As the heir to House Sylvie, her brother already had many things to attend to. Add to that his recent visits to House Coulson, and there was precious little time left for looking after his troublesome sister. This was a very important period in his life, which would decide his future. Cecilia didn't want to be a distraction.

"Fair enough, but you could have asked Oscar to accompany you. He would gladly help you with anything."

"But he seems busy with his own stuff, too. Besides, I'd feel bad asking him for favors when I can't tell him what I'm doing and why."

"I was under the impression you were trying to save your life at all costs—was I mistaken about that?"

Grace glared at her. Cecilia laughed nervously, scratching her cheek.

"Anyway," Grace could see that she was getting nowhere in trying to make Cecilia reflect on her attitude, so she moved on. "We've established that it wasn't the Killer who dropped that flowerpot. I can vouch for that. How do you know it wasn't an accident? Could someone have knocked it down and fled the scene because they were worried about nearly hitting someone?"

"That also crossed my mind at first…"

She thought about the person she glimpsed through the window. She got the impression that they were staring at her with hostility.

Maybe I only imagined it, but that was the vibe I got from them…

If only it had just been an accident. Cecilia certainly hoped nothing like that would happen again.

Grace stopped leaning against the wall.

"Whether the person had ill intent toward you or not, if you want to find them, asking for help is the most efficient way of tracking them down. I'm sure you have a lot of friends who wouldn't mind lending you a hand, so make use of that."

"Yeah, you're right. I'll talk to Gil first."

"Sounds like a plan."

Just as they finished talking, Cecilia felt something make contact with her head, and her vision blurred. No sooner had she realized it was water than an empty bucket struck her head.

"Argh!"

Cecilia dropped to her knees, the metal bucket clanking as she did so. Her body was burning.

"Oww! That water's hot!"

"Are you okay?!" Grace cried out, crouching beside Cecilia. Feeling that the wet ground around her friend was warm, she started checking Cecilia over.

"Did it burn you?!"

"No, it wasn't boiling..."

Cecilia looked up and tried to laugh it off, but her skin looked painfully red.

"Luckily, it doesn't seem serious, but we should get you a cold compress."

Grace scanned the windows directly above where Cecilia had fallen down. She narrowed her eyes suspiciously and spoke in a low voice.

"It would appear that someone is indeed targeting you..."

One day there was a mummified lizard on her desk. Then a rag soiled with milk in her school bag. Another day, her chair was smeared with oil.

It had been a week now since someone started bullying her for reasons unknown. Cecilia was beginning to lose grip on her sanity.

All right, it looks like another day being surrounded by hate!

Finding a piece of paper on her desk with "Die!" written on it, she quickly crumpled it and chucked it into the trash can. Next, she carefully checked her chair and the space under her desk before sitting down. She took out her notebooks and made sure there wasn't anything weird stuck between the pages. She'd only got to the classroom from the dorm, so nobody should have had the chance to sneak anything nasty into her notes yet, and indeed, everything seemed fine this time.

Better to be extra careful, so I don't cut my finger on a shard of glass again.

It would take only a moment of her dropping her guard for her notebooks to be messed with. She had to check them often.

Lastly, she looked all around her seat before allowing herself a breath of relief.

Okay, check complete!

She'd gotten used to it by now. The harassment had become a normal part of her everyday life at school.

Cecilia had stopped walking by the schoolhouse walls with windows and avoided infrequently used paths. She made every effort to never be alone and carried a change of clothes and other spare items she might need.

Of course, she was doing what she could to find the perpetrator. She kept everything she found stuck between the pages of her notebooks as evidence and looked for witnesses whenever something strange occurred. She made a mental list of people who might hold a grudge against her. On a few occasions, she pretended to leave her bag unattended and hid herself nearby, observing it to see if anyone would tamper with it.

Yet despite all that, she still hadn't been able to determine who was playing those cruel pranks on her. Neither had she managed to find a single witness.

How is it possible no one's ever caught them messing with my bag?

It was baffling, yet it kept happening. She had no leads whatsoever.

On another note, she'd also managed to make Gilbert angrier than ever. They had a full-blown fight, worse than anything they'd ever been through before, which ended with Cecilia almost in tears. It really had been a rough week for her, but it hadn't been entirely free of good moments.

"Let's make the most of today!"

"I'll do my best."

"Same."

After school, the resolute Lean was talking to the Machias twins. They were in the empty grounds of Cigogne Orphanage, where Lean's play was to be performed. The carpenters she'd hired were racing to build a stage for her, while Gleick's Theater Company was rehearsing next to them.

The twins had been helping Lean with her production since a few days earlier. House Machias was one of the orphanage's main benefactors, as it turned out. When Eins and Zwei's father had discovered that a play would be shown at the orphanage, he wrote a letter to his sons instructing them to lend a hand.

Not that they obeyed their father's letter immediately—in fact, they'd been ignoring it until Lean heard about it and personally asked them for help.

Among the Gleick's troupe was Cecilia. A conversation she'd had earlier with Lean played back in her mind.

"You don't understand why I insisted that the twins get involved with the play? It's because I thought this would be your chance to get to know them better!

"Besides, why would I say no to two helpers I don't have to pay? For all we know, their dad might even advertise the production for us at no extra cost if we let his progeny do their part to make it all happen.

"It's also fair to assume that House Machias might throw in some extra cash to ensure that this production is up to standard."

That was two, no, three birds with one stone. Lean was going to milk this opportunity dry. As for Cecilia, she was in awe of her friend's greed—*ahem*—fierce business sense.

After the rehearsal, Cecilia decided to rest by the partially erected stage. They weren't in costume yet, but she'd found practice tiring nonetheless. She tasted a salty bead of sweat, which had rolled down her cheek to the corner of her mouth.

I'm so drained...

Suddenly, a shadow fell over her. She raised her head and saw it was Eins, with two wooden mugs in his hands. He held one out toward her, gesturing with his chin for her to take it.

"Oh, thanks!"

She took the beverage, guessing he had been tasked with bringing the actors refreshments. Sure enough, he carried the other mug to another actor nearby.

Well, well, look at him! Eins is being helpful. Who'd have thought?

She followed him with her eyes. Eins had belied her expectations and was doing volunteer work despite his unsociable nature. He didn't seem particularly reluctant, either.

They both had made up since that unpleasant incident. While he still seemed to have some reservations about her, he'd at least apologized for kicking her, and they were on speaking terms. That was progress, and she owed it to Zwei acting as a mediator between them.

"Working hard, Cecil?"

"Not any more than you, Zwei!"

Speak of the devil. Zwei came by to check on her, and she greeted him warmly. While she wouldn't say she was friends with Eins yet, she was getting on well with his brother.

Zwei sat down next to her without her having to ask and gave her a cute grin.

"I saw the rehearsal. You were amazing! If I hadn't known, I'd have assumed you were a professional actor!"

"You really thought so?"

"Yes! You play the role so well that for a moment I forgot you were a boy!"

"Ha-ha-ha..."

Well, there was a reason playing a girl came so easily to her...

Zwei must have taken her laughter for disbelief, for he leaned in closer to gaze at her earnestly.

"I mean it! You're a terrific actor."

"Thanks."

"Do you think I'll do okay? I'm feeling really anxious…"

"You'll be fine, Zwei. I know you can do it!"

"I hope so…"

Besides helping out with odd jobs, Zwei had also gotten a minor role to play, probably as a nod toward his influential father. Since he was rather good-looking, he'd been given quite a lot of lines (although not nearly as many as the main characters) and would be on stage for quite a lengthy period of time during the production. Little wonder that he felt under pressure.

When they asked Eins whether he'd agree to be in the play as well, his answer was apparently *"Over my dead body."*

"And how's it going with your investigation? Have you found out the bully's identity?"

"No, not yet…"

She shook her head. Zwei frowned.

"Who'd be so foolish as to harass you, of all people?"

"Why foolish?"

"Because no villain stands a chance against you! You'd set them straight like this!"

Zwei made a fist and punched the air. He looked adorable doing that, but it bugged Cecilia that he thought of her as some sort of brute.

"Seems to me you've driven someone mad with jealousy."

Cecilia and Zwei looked up simultaneously. Eins stood in front of them with his arms crossed and legs wide apart.

"That's what happens when all you do is chase ass."

"Wait, what…?"

"Tell me I'm not right."

The other twin also had a weird idea about her.

Do I really come off as a womanizer?

The image she'd been trying to craft for herself was that of a gallant prince, so this came as a nasty surprise.

Eins looked away from her in disgust and turned his attention to Zwei. He prodded a box that was in front of him with his foot.

"Anyway, where does this thing go?"

"Oh, this one doesn't go in the storehouse. It needs to be returned to Bobby."

"Bobby? Who's that…"

"He's over there, look. He's wearing a bandana…"

Zwei got up and stood next to his brother, pointing out one of the carpenters to him.

These two are so close…

They were like two halves of a whole. Despite their contrasting personalities, there was always harmony between them, and they cared deeply about each other. They got along not through being similar, but by being different in complementary ways.

"I can't tell which one of the guys you mean. Why don't you *Share?*"

Irritated, Eins raised his voice. Zwei immediately agreed and stretched out his right hand toward his brother. Cecilia saw the Artifact around his wrist. Eins took his brother's hand. Their Artifacts both emitted a faint pulse of light. Then Eins' expression changed.

"Ah, that guy."

"He can be temperamental. Keep that in mind when dealing with him."

"I know that. It's all in there already."

Eins pointed to his head. Cecilia was genuinely amazed.

"That's a useful ability to have! So you can swap memories with each other?"

"Yeah! We can share anything except feelings. We often hold hands for it because it makes it easier, but it's possible without that, too! We can also pull off tricks like this…"

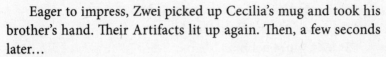

Eager to impress, Zwei picked up Cecilia's mug and took his brother's hand. Their Artifacts lit up again. Then, a few seconds later...

"Wow!"

...an identical cup appeared in Eins' hand. Even the wood grain was exactly the same. Eins put the newly appeared mug down on the ground, looking mildly annoyed.

"There's no need to show that off to people."

"Hee-hee... I got a bit ahead of myself."

Eins scrutinized his brother before lifting the box they talked about earlier off the ground.

"Anyway, I'll take it back to that guy."

"Okay, than—"

A shrill cry cut Zwei off. They all turned in the direction from which it came and took off.

They found a lady lying on the ground, a multitude of props scattered all around her. She must have tripped and dropped a stage kit when she fell. Cecilia pushed past an angry man shouting "Look at the mess you made!" and knelt down by the lady to help her stand up.

"Are you okay? Did you get hurt?"

"No, no, I'm fine. Thank you..."

Seeing that a pretty boy had come to assist her, the lady blushed, but she quickly remembered the pickle she was in. She shook her head to banish her intrusive daydreams.

"The props! Are they okay?!"

"They seem to be."

Cecilia leisurely picked one up to examine it. The props the woman had been carrying were all weapons, like daggers and firearms.

The big man who had been yelling earlier approached them. Cecilia guessed he was the props manager.

"Seriously, how can you be so clumsy?"

"I'm so sorry about this, Zack…"

"At least you're not hurt."

He poked her with a finger. The lady gave an apologetic smile, but seemed slightly pleased for some reason. She started collecting the scattered props and putting them back in the box. Bystanders joined in to help. Cecilia looked closely at the dagger she'd picked up earlier.

"It looks just like the real thing!"

"Real-looking props underpin a top-notch performance! No matter how amazing the acting, if the props look cheap, the audience will be disenchanted."

Cecilia hadn't noticed that Zack was right next to her. He traced the edge of the blade he was holding. Though Cecilia knew that it would not cut him, it made her shudder.

"But I bet it would hurt to get stabbed with it."

"Wanna try?"

She tried to back away, but he mercilessly thrust the blade at her. He didn't just poke her a little, either; he shoved the knife into her belly all the way to the hilt. Cecilia screamed.

"Argh! …Wait, it doesn't hurt?"

"Of course it doesn't. There's a trick to it, obviously."

As he pulled the dagger away from her belly, she realized the blade had retracted into the hilt. It slid back out when it was no longer pressed against her body.

"It's got a spring-loaded mechanism inside. I get these babies from a craftsman I'm friends with. The poor guy's grandkid has recently been giving him trouble with his bad behavior…"

"Aaaaaah!"

They turned, hearing a panicked scream, and saw that Zwei had fallen onto his butt. He'd gone very pale, and he'd fixed his terror-filled eyes on Cecilia.

"Oh, you thought I got stabbed for real? This dagger's just a gimmick."

"...orry."

"What was that?"

"I'm sorry... I'm sorry... I'm sorry..."

"Um, Zwei?"

He cowered on the ground, shaking. Cecilia walked over to him.

"What's wrong? Hey?"

"Aaaaargh! Get away from me!"

He knocked the dagger out of her hand, sending it gliding over the grass. People stared in astonishment. Noticing the look on their faces, Zwei came to his senses and covered his visage in shame.

"I'm so sorry... It's not... I didn't..."

He started hyperventilating and curled up into a tight ball, tears leaking from his eyes as though he was in pain.

"Zwei?!"

"What's happening?"

Eins ran over from the other end of the grounds, where he'd been busy with his chores. As soon as Zwei saw Eins, he fell unconscious.

Half an hour later, Zwei was lying in a bed at the orphanage, asleep. Only Cecilia and Eins, who had brought him there, were in the room with him.

The sun had begun to set, and the last rays of sunshine were falling on Zwei's cheek.

"I'm sorry..."

Cecilia broke the silence.

"What are you apologizing for?"

"Well, this..."

Cecilia dropped her gaze to the floor, feeling pangs of guilt. She didn't mean to, but she had frightened Zwei. It weighed heavily on her conscience now.

When we first met, he also freaked out when he saw the knife...

Back then, she thought he'd just been startled to see a dagger pointed at him, but now she suspected he had some sort of trauma that made him panic at the sight of blades.

She put a blanket over Zwei and started to tuck him in. Just then, she stopped what she was doing and looked at him, surprised.

"Wait a moment..."

"Is something wrong?"

"Didn't your brother have a brooch on his chest?"

Eins gasped and checked Zwei's shirt. The ornament was gone.

"Maybe it fell off when we were carrying him here?"

"I'll go find it."

"Huh?"

Eins' expression darkened, and he turned away from Cecilia.

"I'll find Zwei's brooch. Don't you have another rehearsal to go to?"

"But I want to help!"

Eins was already hurrying to leave, but Cecilia caught up to him.

"I'll be fine on my own!"

He shouted back at her, peevishly.

"I can't leave you like this!"

"Yes, you can! It's not really your business anyway!"

"You'll find it quicker with another pair of helping hands!"

"I don't want your help, is that so hard to unders—"

"It's evening, so we've got to hurry! It'll be impossible to find the brooch when it gets dark! I don't want Zwei to be sad when he wakes up and discovers he's lost it!"

Mentioning his brother seemed to do the trick, and Eins relented.

"Whatever. Do what you want."

"I sure will!"

She wouldn't let his grumpiness put her off. They went out to search for the brooch together.

First, they headed to the spot where Zwei had had the panic attack. It looked different without the props lying all around. The other crew members must have collected them while Cecilia and Eins had been taking Zwei to the orphanage.

Cecilia found the crate where the props had been put away to check whether the brooch might have been mistakenly put in there as well.

"It was an emerald encased in gold, wasn't it?"

"Yes, same as this one."

Eins held out a brooch on his hand. It looked exactly as Cecilia remembered it.

"Ah, you have matching brooches."

"Where we come from, it's customary to give children gemstones matching their eye color as gifts."

"Really? So these brooches have special value to you two? We absolutely have to find Zwei's!"

Cecilia brought her closed hands to her chest in a gesture of concerned determination. Out of the corner of her eye, she saw Eins watching her suspiciously.

"Do people tell you you're weird?"

"Huh? Why would they say that?"

"Because you are."

She was taken aback by that.

"Whatever. Let's keep looking for the brooch!"

His tone had softened a little.

An hour later, they were in the storehouse, which the actors were temporarily using to house various stage props and equipment.

"No luck so far..."

"Yeah..."

They both sighed. It was turning dark outside, and the brightest stars in the sky were already becoming visible. If they continued searching for the brooch, they'd miss dinner at the orphanage.

"By the way... Aren't you going to ask me about Zwei?"

"What about him?"

Cecilia turned away from the area she was searching to face Eins. He'd been staring at her, and now their eyes met.

"About the reason he's terrified of knives and such."

"You'd tell me that?"

"I normally wouldn't, but I don't mind letting you know," he replied in a barely audible whisper.

Cecilia's eyes lit up with curiosity.

"You wouldn't think to use that information for anything weird, anyway. Your mind doesn't work like that."

"...Hey, you're not saying it's because I'm stupid, are you?"

"I meant it as praise."

His tone was still abrasive, but that was what he said. Cecilia could hardly believe her ears.

Eins broke eye contact and bit his lower lip, looking uncharacteristically uneasy.

"Our mother was killed right before his eyes."

"Say what...?"

"You know how twins are considered devil spawn in our parts?"

She remembered Zwei telling her that people had tried to force their parents to kill either him or his brother out of that belief.

"Our father fought back against the superstition, and he got people to shut up about it for a while. But then..."

One night, a particularly superstitious man named Cuddy Miland broke into the Machias residence. He'd worked as a servant there, so he didn't arouse suspicion when he entered the grounds.

He climbed a tree to get into Zwei's room. As chance had it, the twins' mother was in the room with him at the time. When Cuddy tried to stab the boy, she'd shielded him with her own body. The wound she'd suffered was fatal.

"He's been terrified of knives ever since. I suspect he regrets it wasn't him who died then, instead of Mother."

"That's so awful…"

Zwei's past was so shockingly gruesome that Cecilia was at a loss for words. Having his mom stabbed to death right in front of his eyes was simply horrific. But add to that the guilt he must be feeling, knowing that she'd died to protect him…

So that's his secret…

That's what Grace hadn't wanted to tell her. It would've only upset Cecilia if she found out about it from a third party.

"When we gained our special ability, we shared a lot of memories. But he wouldn't share that one with me, no matter how many times I asked."

Eins ran his fingers over his silver bracelet.

"I wish he would. We're two people, but we're also one."

She understood that they'd lived as a single whole. Supporting each other, always. Sharing their experiences, sharing in their suffering. But Zwei wouldn't give Eins access to this one crucial memory, even though the pain attached to it was too much for him to bear—and Eins didn't think it fair.

"Our brooches are mementos of our mother. She chose the gemstones for us," he added quietly, gazing at his emerald brooch.

"So, to be honest, I'm grateful for your help looking for the brooch. It would be really distressing for Zwei to find out he'd lost it."

"If it's so important to him, then we have to find it, no matter what!"

"Yeah. I don't want anything to add to his suffering."

Eins gazed into the distance, grasping his brooch. Cecilia contemplated something for a moment before speaking again.

"You guys are really strong."

"Huh?"

"If I were you, I don't think I'd want to share painful memories if I could avoid it. And if I were Zwei, I don't know how I'd manage to keep all that bottled in and not lose my mind."

"It's my brother who's strong. I don't carry a burden like he does."

"You're selling yourself short. No matter what people say, you're amazing! Really! You do whatever it takes to protect your brother. I know that better than anyone, on account of getting a kicking from you when we first met!"

"Right... Sheesh..."

Eins narrowed his eyes and glared, not wanting to be reminded of that now. Cecilia's smile only widened.

"It must have been so terrible for you to lose your mother, too, but despite that, you put your brother first and look after him. If that doesn't testify to your strength of character, I don't know what does!"

"..."

"I've never experienced the death of a family member myself. There have been some people I've lost touch with, but that's it. But while I obviously don't know what it is like for you, I can imagine it to some extent."

It pained her that she could never again meet the family and friends from her past life as Hiyono. And it was heartrending for her to consider that she'd left them so abruptly, without saying good-bye, to never return. When death separates people, it's hard for both those who are left behind and those who move on to their next life. That was Cecilia's opinion, at least.

"Eins, you're doing so much for your brother—it's incredible!"

A faint blush appeared on his face when she praised him so openly. But for some reason, he grimaced a moment later and turned away from her.

"You're being patronizing!"

"What? I was?"

"Yeah! Did you not even realize how that came off?"

Flustered by his angry growl, she apologized at once, but that didn't pacify him. She looked at him as if searching for something, wondering what was wrong.

It seems I touched a nerve somehow? I didn't mean to sound condescending... I feel terrible for offending him, but I already apologized, and it didn't make a difference. What am I supposed to do...?

"Huh... Ooooh!"

"What the hell?"

Eins covered his ears when she screamed, pointing at something behind him.

"Look! It's there!"

"What?"

"The brooch!"

Zwei's ornament was in a box with imitation jewelry. Someone must have mistaken it for a prop. Cecilia walked over to the shelf and reached up to take the box down but stopped when a burst of pain shot through her shoulder.

"Urgh..."

"It still hurts?"

"Only a little."

She got the box down with Eins' help.

"I'm sorry I injured you. I had no idea it was still bothering you."

"Oh no, it doesn't hinder me much. I can move my arm okay most of the time, it's only when I lift it up that it hurts. Aaand here's the brooch!"

"…"

"Eins, the brooch!"

Overjoyed, she held it out to him, but he refused to look at it. Instead, he grabbed her arms and swore to her in an intense voice:

"I'll make it up to you."

"Huh?"

"I'll take responsibility for what I've done to you."

Just then, she was overcome with a sinking feeling.

"Starting tomorrow, I'll be helping you out at school!"

Oscar's cute fiancée was up to something totally baffling for him yet again.

"Cecil, let me carry that for you."

"It's okay, I can carry it by myself. It's not heavy!"

"No, it's not okay. I'll take it!"

The eldest son of Marquis Machias, Eins, wrangled Cecilia's school bag out of her hand and proceeded to carry both his and hers in one hand as he walked beside her. While Cecilia was at first nonplussed by this, when they started chatting, her usual happy smile returned to her face; she seemed to be enjoying the conversation.

Trailing behind them, Oscar frowned at this unexpected air of comfortable familiarity between Cecilia and Eins.

She did say the other day that she was planning on befriending the Machias twins…

The deadly custard that had given Oscar a three-day-long stomachache was also originally destined for the Machiases. Even Cecilia's appearance at the tea party had only been in service of meeting them.

Well, it looks like she got what she wanted…

Oscar's face darkened as he watched Cecilia laughing at

something Eins said. He didn't want to feel jealous, but he couldn't help it. The pair hadn't noticed him yet and carried on walking down the hallway, so close to each other that their elbows kept touching.

"Eins, are you really okay carrying both bags?"

"Yeah. I'm perfectly fine."

"You don't need to do this, you know…"

"I'm doing this because I owe you for what I did to you."

What had he done to her?

Oscar pricked up his ears. What was Eins talking about? What on earth did he do to Cecilia to now act like her servant?

His thoughts racing, Oscar felt the irresistible urge to act. He quickly caught up to the pair and tapped their backs with a "Hey!" They turned simultaneously.

"Oscar! Hi!"

"Your Highness."

"What's going on here?"

Cecilia blinked, not understanding what he was getting at. Then she noticed that he was looking her bag, which Eins was carrying.

"Ah, this? You see, the thing is that he—"

"I offered to carry it for him."

Eins stepped between Cecilia and Oscar, as if to protect her. Oscar felt a surge of anger at the insinuation that he was of any danger to Cecilia, but his flare of temper lasted only an instant. It was pointless to lose one's nerve over trivial things like that.

He cleared his throat and faced Eins.

"I wasn't accusing you of anything, nor criticizing what you're doing. I was simply curious as to why you're carrying the bag for him. Is it somehow too heavy for Cecil to manage on his own?"

Oscar took the bag from Eins and weighed it in his hand. It was about as heavy as his own, if not lighter. He stared questioningly at Eins, who took a step forward.

"I'm doing what a man should in our situation."

"...What?"

In their situation?

What was he implying? Oscar furrowed his brow. From what he had gathered, Eins had committed some injustice to Cecilia and was trying to make amends for it. But the way he was phrasing it, going on about "their situation" and "what a man should do," struck Oscar as particularly alarming.

No, that can't be! Cecilia wouldn't do something like that. She's too pure! My Cecilia definitely hasn't done anything like that with him!

But now that he'd allowed himself to even consider the possibility, it made him feel so sick that he turned pale. He tried shaking his head to rid himself of the horrible images in his mind, but it was to no avail.

Eins, meanwhile, was oblivious to Oscar's internal turmoil.

"I have to do what I can to prevent any further strain to Cecil's body."

"H-his body?" Oscar exclaimed in a falsetto. Cecilia blushed and ribbed Eins with her elbow.

"Eins, don't say things like that!"

"Why are you embarrassed? I stated a fact."

"Oscar doesn't need to know about it!"

The prince was nearly wheezing at Cecilia's mysterious bashfulness. Eins gazed into her eyes, standing so close to her that it seemed there was more than just friendship between them.

"Does it still hurt?"

"No, of course not! I've been telling you I'm fine!"

"But you said you still felt pain yesterday."

"Yesterday...?" Oscar repeated automatically, struggling to process all the new information. But his voice came out as just a whisper, so the other two didn't hear him.

"Only in that position! And you forced it on me."

"How else would I know if you'd really healed? You wouldn't tell me the truth yourself."

"But…"

"No 'buts.'"

Nothing inappropriate had been said—and the subject of their conversation honestly wasn't anything raunchy—but in his agitated state, Oscar could only take it to mean one thing.

Cecilia finally noticed that he had turned deathly pale. She peered at him with concern.

"Um, Oscar? What's the matter? Are you feeling unwell?"

It was endearing to see her so worried about him. But this wasn't the time to revel in her cuteness. What he'd heard was unforgivable.

He pulled her toward him and addressed Eins, in a tone more menacing than ever before.

"Eins Machias…"

"Yes?"

"Do you realize that you've laid your hands on someone who belongs to another?"

Oscar's voice, as heavy as a black hole, caused Eins to break into a cold sweat.

"What's that about belonging to another?"

Barely a moment after Oscar's threatening question, Gilbert appeared on the scene, swiftly sliding his arm between Oscar and Cecilia to separate them.

"Oh, it's you, Gil."

"Gilbert!"

Her brother pulled Cecilia away from Oscar and beckoned for her to stand behind him, measuring Oscar with a cold look.

"Cecil doesn't belong to anyone. Aren't you getting confused?"

"No, what I meant is—"

"Your statement comes off as quite strange, especially since you have a fiancée, yes? As for me, I know you only meant that Cecil is your friend, but someone else might infer a different sort of relationship between you two from what you said."

Gilbert was essentially saying, *Watch your mouth, or Eins will figure out that Cecil is Cecilia!*

Oscar felt insulted by Gilbert's harsh reprimand, but at the same time, he could see that he was right. Thankfully, Cecilia wasn't the sharpest tool in the shed, or she'd also have realized at this point that Oscar had guessed Cecil's real identity.

Still hiding Cecilia behind him, Gilbert turned to Eins this time.

"And what were you doing, Eins? How many times have I told you to stay away from Cecil? Don't think I've forgiven you for kicking him."

"He kicked you?!"

Oscar looked at Cecilia, appalled. She rubbed the bridge of her nose and giggled uneasily.

"Um, yeah, but he had his reasons. And anyway, we've made up since!"

Cecilia glanced sideways at Eins, who started arguing with Gilbert.

"Get off my case! This has nothing to do with you anyway. It's between me and Cecil, so butt out!"

"Cecil is a very dear friend to me. How could I stand by and idly watch as he starts hanging out with the likes of you—crude, short-fused, and prone to violence? If anyone should get lost, it's you!"

"Look, me kicking him, that's all in the past now, so will you stop bringing it up already?!"

"If it's all in the past, then why are you still clinging to Cecil to 'make up for it'? He said you two have made up already, so that's it, all done. You can leave now and never speak to him again."

"You jerk!"

Verbal sparring wasn't Eins' strength. Unsure of how to counter Gilbert's attack, he stood there quivering with anger, his face red from shame and fury. Oscar, who'd been watching from the sidelines, was pretty impressed.

"It seems that Gilbert won this round."

"Ha-ha… He's always driving Eins away like this…"

So this wasn't the first time? Eins was remarkably persistent… Something suddenly occurred to Oscar, giving him pause.

"Hold on… So the 'thing he'd done to you' that he mentioned earlier, that was him injuring you?" he asked Cecilia.

"Yeah, but I wouldn't call it an injury, it was just a little bruise. He insisted on helping me out until the pain disappears completely, though."

"Now I understand…"

Oscar was overcome with relief. Even though he firmly believed Cecilia wouldn't do anything indecent with another boy, the snippet of conversation he overheard had shaken him to the core.

He glanced at Cecilia with concern.

"So you're not seriously injured?"

"No, no. It did hurt a lot when he kicked me, but I'm all right now!"

She instinctively rubbed her shoulder while saying that.

"And when did that happen, anyway? Recently?"

"Um, it was just after I spoke to Zwei for the first time, and that was at the tea party."

"At the tea party?!"

Oscar lost control of his voice. He'd thought this had happened within the week, but the tea party was over two weeks ago!

"Why didn't you tell me?!"

"Tell you what?"

"That you got hurt! You had so many occasions to mention it to me!"

Cecilia recoiled when he yelled at her. Then she put her fingertips together and said defensively:

"Because it was entirely unrelated to you?"

That sent Oscar's blood pressure skyrocketing. She'd probably meant to say that she didn't want to worry him unnecessarily, but this was yet another case of Oscar being left out of her life, and his patience had been running thin for a while.

"What about Gilbert, did you tell him?"

"Well, yeah. I always tell him everything."

Oscar felt so pathetic that he ground his teeth in powerless anger. Then Cecilia dropped another bomb on him.

"I've been kind of unlucky lately. First that, then the bullying."

"What?!"

"Someone tried to drop a flowerpot on my head, and then I got hit with a bucket full of hot water, and I've been finding nasty things in my school bag…"

Oscar had no idea about any of this. He grasped his head, overwhelmed by just how out of touch he was with what was happening in her daily life.

He overcame the urge to bellow *Why didn't you tell me any of this before?!* and instead firmly took her hands in his.

"Cecil."

"Yes?"

"If something like this happens again, please let me know at once. Tell me if you get hurt. Or if someone is mean to you."

He was so earnest that it threw Cecilia off. She batted her eyelids and looked away guiltily.

"No, I can't bother you with my personal problems. I'm sure you've got plenty of things keeping you busy. Don't worry about me."

"But I—"

With effort, he prevented himself from shouting. He'd achieve nothing by losing his temper and yelling at Cecilia. He gave her hands a squeeze and continued in a calmer voice.

"Do you think me too unreliable to ask for help?"

"What? No…"

"I completely understand that you can't tell me everything. But I…"

But I'm your fiancé!

He couldn't say what he wanted aloud. If she knew he'd seen through her disguise, their relationship would be over.

"But what?"

"But I want you to trust me with your problems. Okay?"

Cecilia looked at him hesitantly, contemplating what he'd said. Oscar tousled her hair to lighten the charged atmosphere.

Fifteen minutes later, they were heading off in separate directions. Gilbert and Cecilia were walking to the dorms together, while Eins, frustrated by having been humiliated by Gilbert, went in the opposite direction. Oscar remembered he had something to get from a classroom, but first, he made a stop at the courtyard.

"Blah…"

Despite not having really done much, he suddenly felt exhausted. He looked down at the ground, having stopped unwittingly. Someone was nearby. Oscar raised his head and called out softly:

"Is that you, Dante?"

Dante materialized as if from thin air.

"You've learned to sense when I'm following you!"

Dante walked up to Oscar from behind and wrapped an arm around his neck. Suddenly, Oscar felt even more tired than before.

"Liar, you wanted me to realize you were there, so you made it easy for me."

"You can tell? I'm so happy that you're beginning to get to know me better."

"If you wanted to talk to me, you could've spared yourself the effort and not hidden in the first place."

"Now, now, where would be the fun in that?"

Oscar sighed, with Dante hanging off his neck.

"Moving on, have you found anything regarding the matter I asked you to investigate?"

"Oscar, my friend, do you think I'd have returned empty-handed?"

"You might, but judging from your good mood, you must have something for me."

"You really do get me so well!"

Dante squeezed Oscar's neck with his elbow so hard that it hurt. Oscar tapped his friend's arm to make him let go. Dante relaxed his grip a little and spoke in a conspiratorial half-whisper.

"Prince Janis has indeed made a move—he's crossed the border into our country by bribing the guards at the northern checkpoint."

"Where did you get this information?"

"From Marlin."

Anger flashed in Oscar's eyes. That was the name of the leader of the assassin syndicate behind Cecilia's abduction a while ago. They'd managed to catch Marlin after she was wounded, but *someone* interfered, so she escaped in the end.

Marlin had since let her men go and disbanded Heimat, but the whole affair put Oscar in a difficult position. To save his reputation, he'd needed to cover up the fact that to save Cecilia, he had commandeered fresh recruits who hadn't completed their basic military training and weren't ready for deployment, on top of failing to capture the leader of the syndicate. That's why he'd needed to write in his report that Cecil had single-handedly defeated Heimat and rescued Cecilia, a legendary feat if it were true. He silently cursed Marlin for giving him so much grief.

"I was under the impression you had cut ties with them."

"Well, I'm no longer a member of Heimat, but Marlin and the other ex-members are like family to me!"

Dante stuck his tongue out at the glaring Oscar. Though he felt a bit guilty over associating with Marlin after all she'd done, that wasn't going to stop him.

"Don't worry, I'll see to it that nobody catches wind of it. We can't have the public discover that their future king's best friend used to be a despicable cutthroat, right?"

Dante had told him earlier that the real Hamptons now lived abroad. The nearly ruined baron and his family had been paid a very generous sum to transfer their family name and rank to Dante. Since they'd been struggling for some time, they hadn't been socializing with other nobles, so nobody really knew them. This had allowed Dante to easily take the place of the Baron's real son. Huey had acquired his new identity in a similar manner.

"I trust you can cover your tracks well. But I'll have to see to it that noble houses are periodically verified so as not to allow more assassins to take on someone else's identity."

"You're going to make life more difficult for my old friends."

"Tell them to be patient, and they might find employment in my service one day."

There were two reasons for Oscar not being too keen on having the troops at his command search for the ex-Heimat assassins. One being that they were Dante's de facto family, and the other that he was planning to have them work for him someday. What king wouldn't dream of having his own secret unit of highly skilled soldiers capable of carrying out assassinations?

"I'm afraid they already have their schedule filled for the foreseeable future."

"Who hired them?"

Oscar's eyes narrowed. Depending on who had hired them, he might have to defang them before they became a threat to him. Dante noticed his wariness and gave him a laid-back smile.

"Nobody you should be worried about. A certain duke's son."

"...Gilbert?"

Dante's playful grin confirmed Oscar's suspicion.

"Marlin was impressed that he'd managed to locate and contact them without needing to go through me. He's been secretly searching for them ever since that kidnapping, as it turns out."

Dante unwrapped his arm from Oscar's neck and pirouetted around to face him.

"He's still studying, so it will be a while before he takes over as the head of his house, but he's been exchanging correspondences with Marlin. She's looking forward to working for him. The fact that he's so close with Cecil will make things even more interesting."

"Well, he got one out from under me."

Yet Oscar didn't seem bothered, certain as he was that Gilbert would not use the assassins against him. Dante, on the other hand, pouted in displeasure.

"Why did you want them anyway? I'm more useful to you than Marlin and her crew. Any intel they get soon trickles down to me, and if we fought, I'd certainly come out on top. I'm worth more than all of them combined!"

"I know that."

"Oh, you do?" Dante crooned, pleased with Oscar's immediate agreement. He put his arm around the prince's neck again.

"Still, it's alarming that Prince Janis has come over here, isn't it? Considering all the terrible stories about him."

"Let's hope he's merely on a sightseeing trip."

A deep crease appeared on Oscar's forehead as he frowned.

It was less than a week until Advent. Cecilia was sitting in a room in Cigogne Orphanage, facing a mirror. However, the reflection staring back at her was unfamiliar.

Her face had been powdered to look as white as fine porcelain, while her eyes were accentuated with bewitching purple eyeshadow. She wore a blond wig, its locks reaching past her waist, and a white dress—not of the extravagant type noblewomen wore to balls, but one with a simple, modest design. The gauzy fabric gave her an ethereal aura.

"And that's it!"

"Yikes…"

Cecilia was rather crestfallen. Behind her stood Lean, enormously pleased with the results of her work.

"Well, how do you like your stage costume and makeup? Amazing, am I right?"

"It's beautiful, but are you sure it doesn't make it obvious that I'm a girl?"

"Nah, no one will suspect a thing! So get ready for the dress rehearsal. Make sure you don't step on the hem and rip the dress off you."

"I'll be careful…"

Cecilia examined herself in the mirror again, still feeling nonplussed about the whole thing. Needless to say, she looked one hundred percent like a girl. With this makeup on, she didn't resemble Cecil at all, but neither did she look like her real self, so maybe things would be okay after all.

She left the room with Lean, and they headed outside to the open-air stage. Cecilia took this opportunity to ask Lean about something that had been nagging at her for a while.

"So you really didn't mention anything about this show to Oscar and Gilbert?"

"Yup, and right up to the big day, I intend to keep it a secret from everyone at the academy. Please make sure you don't let it slip, especially to those two!"

"Right up to the big day? So you ARE going to tell people about it on the day?"

"Oops, you caught me."

Lean seemed mildly surprised that Cecilia had figured that out. If she made it known that Cecil would be starring in a play, it was only natural that a lot of students would turn up to see it. Cecilia hadn't thought to ask Lean if she was selling tickets to the show, but if she did, then this would be a big boost to sales. And that, of course, would appeal to Lean's money-grubbing tendencies.

When Lean had reassured her that *"Students from the academy wouldn't turn up at the orphanage for no reason, and without anyone announcing your name, the audience won't know who you are!"* what she really meant was that she would invite the students and tell them it was Cecil in the lead role.

But then why would she insist on not telling Oscar and Gilbert about the play?

"Why not tell Oscar and Gil that we're doing this show? If you're eventually going to invite students from the academy anyway, what's the problem with telling everyone now? That way you may get more people to come."

"Oh, are you trying to tell me you want Oscar and Gilbert to see you on stage?"

"Not really, but they'll be mad at me for not keeping them in the loop when they do find out."

She could picture Gilbert getting so worked up about it that his veins would pop out. And Oscar...he'd probably make that pitiful face at her again.

"I'll tell them on the day of the play. I only want to keep it a secret for now."

"But why?"

"I want it to be a surprise!"

Lean touched her lips with her index finger, smiling. She was definitely up to something weird, but Cecilia had no way of dragging out the truth from her.

"I've told you this many times, but you can relax. There's no danger to you, honestly. Just don't tell those two. That's all I'm asking."

"Yeah, okay."

Cecilia nodded in the end. Whatever it was her friend was hiding, she had no solid grounds to object to her request.

The girls left the orphanage. In front of the affiliated church was the large stage, complete at last. Children from the orphanage were playing around it, and occasionally, they would stop playing to greet Lean. It made for a heartwarming scene.

"By the way, what's the deal with Zwei?"

"What do you mean?"

"Since that time he passed out, only Eins has been coming to help. I'm getting really worried, you know, and asking Eins about him is no use. He just makes an unfriendly face at me and says his brother is fine."

Cecilia smiled briefly, thinking how typical it was of Eins to clam up like that. She decided it was okay to briefly explain the situation to Lean.

"Zwei hasn't been feeling well since. He's still coming to his classes, but he hasn't had the energy for the show. But Eins said this morning that he'll turn up today!"

"Cool. That will be your chance!"

"Huh? Chance for what?"

Lean pointed at Cecilia, stopping her finger right in front of her nose.

"For you to earn some affection points! You've got to raise their fondness for you at the same rate, right? So you'd better work on Zwei!"

"But I'm already good friends with him," Cecilia protested, and Lean gave her a bemused look.

"You think? To me it looks like you're really close with Eins... Kind of like, he might have a crush on you?"

Lean made a heart with her hands. Cecilia frowned.

"No way. Why do you always fantasize about guys falling in love at the first sign of them getting along?"

"You think it's only in my imagination?"

Lean interlaced her arm, pouting.

"Not to sound too philosophical, but it's impossible to really know what's in another person's head. What are they thinking, how do they feel about this or that? What do they like or hate, or what triggers them? Without being able to see the twins' affection gauges like in the game, keeping them at an equilibrium requires a sixth sense. Completing their routes is hella hard."

Lean's off-hand remark left Cecilia deeply unsettled.

"And what she said really got to you?"

"Yeah."

Cecilia nodded, a sandwich in her hand. The day after Lean unwittingly gave her an anxiety attack, she met up with Gilbert for lunch in the greenhouse as usual. Gilbert had finished his food first and was perusing a difficult-looking book.

"What do you think, Gilbert?"

"Hmm. From what I've seen, both twins seem fond of you, but I can't really tell if one cares for you more than the other. Plus, appearances can be deceiving. Sometimes people act like they like you even when they hate your guts."

"Yeah, that's possible, too…"

She bit into her sandwich, looking stressed. Through the glass ceiling, she could see the clear autumnal sky, as serenely beautiful as ever.

"You've got to rely on your own reading of the twins' feelings for you. Nobody can give you a definite answer as to how much they like you."

"Right…"

She had to agree with him there. Outside of games, it was impossible to know how someone was feeling for certain. You could only guess at the thoughts, feelings, and emotions of other people based on their actions. Gilbert was right—she had to trust her own gut and see where that got her.

Except that I'm terrible at noticing people's feelings. I might accidentally say something insensitive without even realizing it…

Cecilia was more or less aware of her poor observation skills. She was the only person in her household who hadn't clued into the fact that Hans the soldier was dating Sharon the maid. While it had been glaringly obvious to everyone but her, Cecilia had just thought they seemed to get along.

I don't even know what Gilbert's thinking, to be honest…

She looked at her brother sitting next to her, absorbed in his book. He was an introvert, which made it all the more difficult to read him. He would laugh or get angry sometimes, and though he cried when he was little, he generally wore a neutral expression. Cecilia never knew what was going on in his head.

I don't even know what he's planning to do regarding the Coulsons…

His biological family wanted to take him back, but would he agree? He'd revealed nothing of his intentions to Cecilia, and she couldn't guess which way he was leaning. She didn't want him to leave, but she wasn't even sure if telling him her thoughts on this was the right thing to do. Since he hadn't discussed that with her, she figured he didn't care for her opinion.

"What is it? Do I have something stuck on my face?"

Gilbert looked up from his book, noticing her staring at him. She looked away, abashed.

"Um…"

"Why don't you tell me what's eating away at you?"

When she didn't readily reply, he added:

"When you keep things to yourself, things always go wrong."

Cecilia's eyes darted left and right as she wondered whether it was okay for her to ask the question. The fact that he never mentioned to her that the Coulsons wanted him back could mean that he didn't want to talk about it or that he preferred she didn't know about this matter. But Gilbert being Gilbert, he might have simply thought it not worth mentioning or have forgotten to tell her.

"Why are you hesitating? Out with it."

"Gilbert, um…"

He looked at her intently, waiting for her to continue. She straightened up and faced him, deadly serious.

"I heard that the Coulsons asked you to move back in."

"Who told you?"

"Lean… I mean, she told me the rumors."

"Right…"

Gilbert was surprised at first, but then nodded, confirming that the stories were true. Cecilia clenched her fists in her lap.

"And I've been wondering…if you were going to say yes?"

"So that's been bugging you, huh?"

"I cannot deny it, yes."

She replied with uncharacteristic formality, maybe because she was so stressed. Gilbert contemplated her for a moment before softening his expression.

"Let me put your mind at ease. I won't leave your side. I promise."

"You mean it?"

"Of course."

The tension in her body dissipated. So he was more averse to the idea of leaving the Sylvies than she'd realized.

"Yay! I'm so happy to hear that!"

Relieved, she beamed at him, and he smiled back at her. He seemed rather happy, too.

Hold on... Something's odd...

Something wasn't right. She couldn't quite put her finger on it, but Gilbert's reply bugged her somehow. She sensed that he'd left something unsaid.

"Cecilia, dear..."

"Hmm? Yes?"

She snapped out of her wonderings.

What did he call me just now?

He wouldn't normally use terms of endearment like that when talking to her. Had she imagined that? Noticing her blinking in confusion, he said it again.

"Cecilia, dear."

"Um, yes?"

"I love you."

"That's nice... Wait, what?"

His tone was perfectly casual, but the way he'd addressed her was very unusual. It made what followed sound a bit different from reaffirming his brotherly affections for her.

Did he mean...?

She felt bewildered, and her ears grew hot. She didn't understand why he'd worded what he said that way. Not caring to explain himself, Gilbert stood up from the table. Normally, Cecilia would have followed, but all strength left her body as she struggled to process what just happened. She glanced up, and her eyes met Gilbert's. He seemed pleased to see the effect he'd had on her.

"Shall we get back to the classroom?"

"Uh, yeah, sure."

She managed to get the words out somehow. When he offered her his hand to help her stand up, she took it. Somehow, his hand felt colder than usual.

✦ CHAPTER 4 ✦ Advent

Orange lanterns dotted the lawns. Spiderwebs and dust bunny-themed decorations swayed in the gentle breeze. Black pennants appeared on rooftops, while imitation skulls lurked on the wayside.

People were dressed in either black robes or garments made from a patchwork of old pieces of fabric and had blackened their faces with soot or dyed them with crushed berries. Some of the children running around were wearing wooden masks.

It was the twenty-fourth of October, the beginning of the Week of Ashes—the first part of Advent. Although this holiday had plenty of unique elements, it was this world's version of Halloween.

"I knew it would end up like this..."

Standing by the arched gateway outside Vleugel Academy, Lean stared with resignation at the resplendent white horse-drawn carriage parked there. She was dressed in a heavy white robe, signifying that she was a Holy Maiden. Next to her stood Cecilia, in a black outfit resembling a military uniform. The coachman had left to fill out some paperwork.

Cecilia patted Lean's shoulder to cheer her up.

"Some things can't be helped."

"You're one to talk."

"All I'm saying is that it's part of the game's scenario."

Cecilia laughed nervously. Lean pouted and looked away. Of course, she'd known this would happen since that's how it goes in the game.

One of Prosper Kingdom's Advent traditions was that the Holy Maiden and one of her knights would parade around the capital city of Algram. The incumbent Holy Maiden was unable to perform this duty due to her poor health this year, so it fell to Holy Maiden candidate Lean to play that part.

"You should be doing this by yourself, Cecilia. I don't even have a single Artifact, and I haven't raised anyone's affection to a significant level anyway!"

"But to the public, I'm a knight, not a potential Holy Maiden."

"It should be you according to the game's rules! This just isn't fair!"

Lean pulled a face, fed up with this whole parade business.

In the game, Advent is a special event that falls at the midpoint of the story. In it, the Holy Maiden candidate with the highest total affection points gets to ride in the carriage with one of her knights to stand in for the infirm official Holy Maiden. The knights take turns accompanying the maiden over the seven days of the Week of Ashes and the seven days of the Week of Light.

This important task keeps Lean busy for two, maybe three hours a day, but after that, she is free to do whatever she wants since there is no school during the holiday. If the protagonist has a high affection level with the accompanying knight, he invites her out on a date. If she agrees, this triggers a special date event.

As it happened, the knight Lean was paired with for the first day of the Week of Ashes was Cecil.

"And anyway, why are you wearing this outfit? What happened to the one I made you? This is what Gilbert wore in the game! Why didn't you put on the vampire costume? It would have looked way better on you than this!"

"I didn't have a choice. They gave me this and told me to put it on."

"But what about my hard work making you a unique costume?!"

"I'm sorry I couldn't wear it."

Cecilia's apology wasn't enough to banish Lean's bad mood, though. Advent is an event where the maiden spends time with the knights, but Lean was more interested in Huey than any of the official love interests, so it was just a chore to her. She huffed and crossed her arms. That seemed to calm her down a bit, though she still looked rather disgruntled.

"Whatever! I guess I'll have to put up with this before we get to the fun part."

"What fun part? What are you planning for after this?"

"That's a secret."

Lean pressed her index finger to her lips, the very picture of a charming heroine of a romance story.

And so, the first day of the Week of Ashes celebrations had begun...

"Ooh! It's Prince Cecil!"

"Goodness, he's so handsome in this uniform! He's gorgeous!"

"What a feast for the eyes! Oh no, I think I might faint!"

"Pull yourself together, Samantha!"

Er... I don't think this is how it's supposed to go?

Cecilia sat in the carriage with a frozen expression as people cheered, excited to see her. She was used to being the center of attention, but this was some next-level adoration.

"Is that the boy you mentioned earlier?"

"Yes, that's him. The hero from this novel was based on him, did you know? My daughter's obsessed with Cecil!"

"My, he's drop-dead gorgeous! If only I were younger and wasn't married!"

"Oh, he looked at me! The prince looked at me!"

"After finally seeing him in person, I've got to say, he's cute. Just my type."

"Same. If he ever comes to our bar, I'll make him forget about men. It's a waste, really."

"Hey now, the fact he's that way in the novel doesn't mean he's like that in reality. You shouldn't assume."

"Let's invite him to our place after this and see for ourselves."

"Oh my goddess, he's superb! I've never seen anyone so exquisite in my life!"

"I only learned the other meaning of 'bottom' and 'top' from Madame Neal's novel, but I just can't agree with her! Honestly! He just screams 'bottom' to me!"

"That's all right, Kay. Madame Neal wouldn't judge you for thinking he's moe. Your feelings are valid, it's all down to personal interpretation! We can all love him in different ways!"

From moms to BL enthusiasts, everyone was swooning over Cecil. It wasn't just students from the academy. Cecilia found this highly alarming. She spotted the infamous BL novel in the hands of many onlookers.

Cecilia moved her head slowly, starting and stopping like a windup toy, until she faced Lean.

"Explain."

"I wasn't expecting a reaction like this, I swear..."

Lean brought her hands to her cheeks anxiously.

"It would seem that people somehow found out you were the model for Ciel…"

"*Somehow*, huh…?"

Ciel was one of the protagonists of Lean's story. He was the top. The other main character, Oran, was based on Oscar. He was a bottom.

Cecilia's fellow students had easily deduced who served as the inspiration for Ciel, but the people loudly commenting on her looks now were mostly common city folk. The Vleugel kids were nobles, and the aristocracy didn't mingle with the commoners, so how could have this piece of information got out?

"Wonderful works of art unite people regardless of their social class!"

That sounded deep. If it only weren't for the fact that Lean was shamelessly praising her own novel, which turned out to be very inconvenient for Cecilia.

Lean kept smiling at the people they were passing by as she whispered to Cecilia.

"This is actually a splendid opportunity."

"For what?"

"You see, I think that anime beats manga every time."

"Sorry, what?"

That reference to pop culture from their past lives completely blindsided her.

"Movies and theater performances are also good. A story presented on paper can only go so far. You get so much more out of watching the characters moving and talking."

"Okay…"

Cecilia stared at her friend with a wrinkled brow, still unsure what her friend was getting at. Lean, however, was in a world of her own now, and she continued passionately.

"That got me thinking, and I've arrived at the conclusion that I must make every effort to bring your character out of the pages of a book and into the three-dimensional world! We need to make this a thing!"

"Whaaaat?"

"Imagine the possibilities! You will be a living story, everything you do giving rise to new interpretations! People will start writing their spin-off fiction based on what they observe!"

"I don't want that! Seriously! It would make my life hell!" Cecilia pleaded with tearful eyes. Lean, on the other hand, laughed without an ounce of compassion.

"The die is cast!"

"Stop it! Why don't you ask me what I think first?!"

"By the way, the second issue of my magazine is coming out soon!"

"Why do you always spring things on me like that?!"

Tears were nearly spilling out of Cecilia's eyes onto her face. If people weren't looking, she'd break down into sobs.

"Guess what it's going to be about. *Ciel gets scouted to star in a play...in a female role! Crow falls in love, thinking Ciel really is a girl, but Oran keeps him in check!* Sounds good, no?"

"That sounds awfully familiar, Lean!"

"Really? What a coincidence."

Cecilia grabbed her friend by the shoulders and shook her.

"That was the real reason you wanted me in the play, wasn't it?! You're going to cash in on it and use the show to sell your fiction!"

"Don't you think the fans will love seeing a scene from the story happen in real life?"

Lean was all smiles, while Cecilia was fuming. They were probably making the coachman uncomfortable. Although he wouldn't be able to hear what they were talking about due to the din of the crowd, their agitated voices made it obvious that they were arguing.

Lean didn't seem concerned about that as she pointed her index finger upward, adding with a smile:

"I actually had one more fantastic idea—"

As Lean kept monologuing, Cecilia noticed a round white object flying at them. It was going to hit Lean square in the back of her head.

"Lean! Duck!"

Cecilia put her hands on her friend's shoulders and pushed her down to get her out of harm's way. The object hit her instead.

"Argh!"

The object struck Cecilia on the head. She heard a crack, and then something slimy began dripping down her hair.

At least it didn't hurt...

"Are you okay?!"

Lean, still in Cecilia's arms, poked her head up in alarm. She freed herself from Cecilia's embrace and carefully looked her up and down.

"What's this goo? Don't tell me someone's thrown an egg at us?"

"It was an egg, yeah."

Cecilia gave a baffled response as the egg dribbled down her head. She was pretty sure she'd made out the back of the person who threw the egg. It was a boy, around the same age as her. He was dressed in a black Advent outfit, and she quickly lost sight of him as he blended in with the crowd. Then she noticed Eins and Zwei standing where the other boy had been, but they certainly didn't have anything to do with him.

"Do you think it was the same person who's been bullying you who threw the egg?"

"Could be." Cecilia nodded.

"Sorry. He got away."

Eins apologized when Cecilia got off from the carriage. Zwei was next to him, panting heavily.

"We almost got him, but with everyone dressed the same, he disappeared into the crowd…"

"He had the hood of his cloak up, so we couldn't see his face."

"Unfortunately."

Beads of sweat glistened on their foreheads. They must have given the egg-thrower a good chase. Cecilia felt a bit guilty.

"Don't worry. Thank you for trying to catch him."

"He was right next to us, so of course we couldn't ignore it."

"But we failed to catch him in the end."

"You always focus on negatives, Zwei."

"I'm just stating a fact."

A sad, disarming smile appeared on Zwei's lips. Eins glanced at him before turning back to Cecilia. He wiped egg white off her cheek with the back of his finger.

"Anyway, we've got to help each other out, right? It's so nasty that someone would egg you. Are you okay?"

"Yeah, sure, it was nothing!"

Her wig and costume needed a wash, but she was unhurt. Lean piped up.

"But what are we to do now? Lord Cecil is in no state to continue the parade after this attack. Why don't we call it off for the rest of the day?"

Lean shot a glance at the guards at the back. There were four of them. They'd also given chase to the egg-thrower, but they couldn't get through the crowd fast enough, so they came back empty-handed. The look Lean gave them was frigid, as if she no longer trusted their ability to protect her from anything.

"I could politely ask if it's okay for us to just go home for the day."

"Why don't you let me accompany you for the rest of the parade?"

The unexpected offer came from Eins.

"Sorry, but what did you just say?"

"I even happen to have the right outfit for it."

He parted his ashen cloak to reveal a military uniform similar to Cecilia's. While the knights' outfits varied slightly in design, they all shared the same basic aesthetic.

"I didn't need to wear it today, but I had no other black clothes."

"Isn't that lucky?"

Cecilia noticed that Zwei was also wearing his black uniform under the cape. It seemed to be exactly the same as his brother's.

Eins removed his cloak, giving it to Zwei, who put it over Cecilia's shoulders. He gently ushed her forward.

"Eins will take care of the parade duties. You should go back to the dorm so you can get changed into fresh clothes. I'll walk you there."

"Huh? You don't need to! It's not like I don't know the way. I wouldn't want you to waste your time."

She shook her head firmly. Eins, who was just getting into the carriage, turned to her in irritation.

"Don't be dumb. That egg guy may still be around, so let Zwei walk you back without making a fuss."

"I agree, you should go together. It's too risky for you to be left alone, Lord Cecil!"

Lean sided with Eins, her voice sweetly innocent. Zwei smiled at Cecilia and gave her a pleading look. She had to give in.

"Okay then, I'll go with Zwei. Thank you all!"

Lean and the two boys exchanged glances and grinned, assured this was the right call.

Cecilia and Zwei walked back through the city. Even though this was the Week of Ashes, the atmosphere on the streets was still lively, probably because it was only the first day of Advent observances. People were dressed in blacks and grays, and many were smiling.

"Come to think of it, I never thanked you," Zwei said to Cecilia as they turned off the busy main road into a back alley.

"For what?"

"For finding my brooch."

Her mind had been elsewhere, so she didn't know what he was talking about at first. He pointed to the emerald-green brooch on his chest. It was the one Zwei had dropped the day he fainted, which she and Eins looked for together.

"My brother told me you found it. This brooch is really important to me, so I'm so glad it didn't get lost."

"It wasn't just me, Eins was also—"

"Thank you from the bottom of my heart, Cecil!"

He talked over her. She felt it would be awkward to correct him at this point so she let it go with a "Glad I could help..."

Did Eins not share his memories with Zwei?

This struck her as a bit strange, since she was under the impression that they regularly shared all their memories. *Maybe they don't sometimes.* She decided not to dwell on it.

Zwei fixed his gaze on the horizon.

"You're a real hero. You're strong, kind, funny, and weird."

"...Weird?"

"I meant that in a good way!"

Despite that assertion, Cecilia wasn't quite sure what "being weird in a good way" was supposed to be and whether she should be happy to be called that.

"That must be why even Eins likes you."

"Yeah?"

"He may not look it, but he's actually very shy. Much more than me."

Cecilia opened her eyes wide in surprise. Zwei noticed her reaction but didn't turn to her.

"He wasn't like that when we were little. But then someone betrayed him, and he stopped trusting people."

"Who betrayed him?"

"A servant who worked for our family for a long time. We called him Uncle Cuddy."

"Oh!"

She remembered the conversation she'd had with Eins previously about their mother's killer, Cuddy Miland, who was a servant at their house.

Zwei made big eyes at her, surprised by her reaction.

"Has Eins told you about him?"

"Um... Well..."

"You can't lie, can you?"

There was a twinge of sorrow in his laugh as he turned his face away from her again, looking straight ahead.

"It's not a big deal. Everybody knows about it back home. It wasn't a secret."

"Still, I'm sorry..."

"You don't need to apologize for anything."

Zwei laughed nervously and stared at the ground.

"Anyway, Eins used to really like that servant. Cuddy taught him how to ride a horse and care for it. But then, he..."

Zwei didn't need to finish. Cecilia knew what happened— Cuddy broke into Zwei's room and attacked him. Their mother had managed to save him, but she was killed in the process.

"Eins never got along with our father. Dad has been very strict with him and has saddled him with high expectations; he's the firstborn, so he'll be the heir. That's why Eins bonded with Cuddy so much. He was like a father to my brother."

Zwei bit his lower lip.

"Since then, Eins has lost all faith in people. Even though..."

Zwei's quiet voice faded into silence. Cecilia tentatively finished his sentence for him.

"Even though he's a people person by nature?"

Zwei raised an eyebrow.

"You can tell?"

"Kind of, yeah."

"So you get that about him…"

She couldn't quite read the emotion on Zwei's face after he said that. Was it loneliness? Bitterness? Astonishment? Whatever it was, pain flashed in his eyes for a moment before his usual gentle air soon returned.

"Well, here we are."

Zwei looked up at the schoolhouse surprised, as if he hadn't realized when they'd arrived, so engrossed he was in their conversation. He extended his hand toward her.

"I'm always happy to help if you need it."

"Um, thanks."

She shook his hand. He flashed her a little smile before saying "bye" and turning back to return to the parade route.

The campus, which typically bustled with students, was deserted during Advent celebrations. Some went out in the city to take part in the festivities, while those who had no interest in Advent traditions went back home for this additional vacation after the all-too-brief summer break.

Cecilia entered the empty campus and headed for her dorm. She walked slowly, lost in thought.

Zwei seemed kind of down…

Of course, she couldn't really expect him to cheerfully recount the most traumatic event of his past. It made perfect sense that he'd been giving off sad and anguished vibes when he was telling the story, but there was something else that gave her pause. An emotion she couldn't quite put her finger on, which kept nagging at her.

Well, I don't know… Maybe it's all in my head?

"What are you doing here?"

Cecilia turned. Oscar had come up to her.

"Hi, Oscar! And you? Have you already been to the parade?"

"No, I haven't. My father had called me to see him."

If his father, the king, asked him to come over, that meant Oscar had to oblige. Even though the palace was in the same city, it took more than an hour to get there by horse-drawn carriage. The prince's life was so busy.

"But why are you here? Today's your turn to accompany Lean."

"Ha-ha, you won't believe it, but someone threw an egg at me."

"What?"

"I'm thinking it might have been the same person who's been playing nasty pranks on me at the academy."

She parted her cloak to show him her egg-splattered outfit underneath. Oscar frowned. She then recounted everything that had happened that day in detail—it took only a minute or so—and he furrowed his brow even more.

"The guards have failed in their duty."

"You can't really blame them. The Church picked them out. They probably haven't had much training."

"It's no excuse. I'll make a formal complaint. I would lend some of our guards, but I don't know whether the Church would agree to that."

Holy Maidens were under protection of the Church of Caritade, which wasn't officially connected to the bureaucracy of the Kingdom of Prosper. Though church and state were ostensibly separate to ensure freedom of faith for every citizen, ninety percent of the population were followers of the Church of Caritade. It was a national religion in all but name. This was evinced by the fact that the king was required to respect the authority of the Holy Maiden, who stood atop the Church of Caritade's hierarchy. The government had also made Advent, Caritade's biggest religious observation, a national holiday and allowed the Selection Ceremony to be held at Vleugel Academy.

"I fully expect them to tell me to keep my nose out of their affairs."

"That's hypocritical, considering that without the support of the royals and nobles, the Church wouldn't even be able to make a big thing out of Advent."

Oscar rubbed his forehead at Cecilia's remark. The ambiguous relationship between the royals and the Church was probably giving the crown prince a headache already.

"Well, enough about that. Were you going to the dorm to get changed?"

"Yeah. I don't want people to see me like this."

"I'll go with you."

Cecilia widened her eyes, thrown by yet another guy offering to walk her somewhere that day. Oscar explained patiently.

"The person who threw the egg at you is almost certainly a student here, correct? They might be plotting to ambush you when you go to get changed. I'll walk you to your room and wait outside while you put on a fresh change of clothes."

"That's very considerate, but are you sure you don't mind?"

"Absolutely. I had nothing else planned for the rest of the day anyway."

In reality, Oscar must've had a ton of things on his plate, but he'd put that all aside for the time being. He faced the direction Cecilia was going.

"Okay, if you say so! Thanks!"

"Uh-huh," Oscar murmured.

Cecilia got changed in her room while Oscar stood guard outside. Thankfully, her wig looked presentable after a quick wipe-down, but the military uniform and Eins' cape were in need of a more thorough cleaning.

The wig could do with a proper wash, too. I should forget about going back and stay in the dorm for the rest of the day...

She had been looking forward to the annual Advent festivities, but considering the circumstances, she'd have to give part of the first day a miss.

As she was putting on a clean shirt, she called out to Oscar.

"You're the prince, but here I am making you act like my body-guard. I feel kind of bad..."

"Don't worry about it. I want to keep you safe because I love you, and my position has nothing to do with it."

He said it matter-of-factly, but his words made Cecilia freeze. Suddenly, her cheeks were burning up. She replied in an unnatural voice:

"Th-that was very direct."

"Is there something wrong with being direct?"

"It's just that... Most people wouldn't be so open about that."

She buttoned her shirt, grateful that they were separated by the door. Then she gathered up courage to ask something that had been on her mind for a while.

"So Oscar, I'm, um, a guy like you..."

"And?"

"And since I'm a guy, I was just wondering if you like me for who I am or if maybe you're just curious about...experiences with boys because of that story Lean wrote?"

"What."

The anger and disbelief in his voice caused her to shrink back. She was thinking frantically of something to say when he went silent, but before she could come up with anything, he sighed loudly and spoke to her again.

"You want to know my sexual orientation?"

"Um, er...yeah?"

"Did you think I confessed my love for you simply because I like men and you happen to be a guy?"

That wasn't really it. She didn't think that Oscar would hit on anyone just because they were a pretty boy like Cecil. What she was trying to establish was whether Oscar was into girls in addition to guys.

She heard him sigh again.

"Let me put it like this…"

"Yes…?"

"It's only a thought experiment on my part, mind you."

He sure was beating around the bush.

"If you were a girl, I'd have fallen for you all the same."

"…"

"In some ways, it would make things easier. You wouldn't have doubts about my intentions, for example."

Cecilia put a hand to her chest, his answer skimming over her secret. Sensing her disquiet perhaps, Oscar sighed yet again and spoke to her in a gentle tone.

"Gender may initially play a role in whether I notice someone as a potential romantic interest, but once I'm in love with someone, their gender becomes meaningless. At least that's how it is for me."

"Oscar…"

"I love your sometimes excessively uncompromising sense of justice, your honesty, your cheerfulness, your endearing kindness, your innocence…"

He paused to take a breath.

"And the carefree way you smile at me."

"…"

"What I like about you has nothing to do with your gender."

"I see…"

She managed to squeeze an answer out of her tightened throat. His earnest declaration of all the things he loved about her made her ears, cheeks, all of her body feel hot. She didn't check in the mirror, but she wondered if she'd turned red all over.

"Have you finished getting changed, Cecil?"

"Um, yeah."

"Let me come in, then."

"N-no, wait!"

She had put on her clothes, and her wig was in place, but she'd be embarrassed for Oscar to see her crimson from emotion. She lunged at the door to stop Oscar from coming in, but he opened it so swiftly that she ended up bumping into him.

"S-sorry!"

She tried to pull away at once, but he wrapped his arms around her. He held her close, like he didn't want her to leave his embrace, with one hand on her back and the other on the back of her head.

I never knew a heartbeat could be so loud...

But was it her own or Oscar's? Or maybe both? They were so close that she couldn't tell.

Oscar's serious address turned her attention away from trying to solve that mystery.

"Take all the time you need, but please do some soul-searching regarding how you feel about me. And don't focus on irrelevant details like gender or my position."

"I will..."

"Can you promise me that? Because I don't want to hear excuses along the lines of, *Oh, but wouldn't it be weird, since we're both guys?* again."

"I—I promise! I'll figure out how I feel about you!"

Oscar relaxed his embrace when she shouted her vow, gripping onto his clothes. Then he moved his hand from the back of Cecilia's head and stroked her hair to calm her.

"I'll leave now. Keep your eyes open and be on your guard until we find the person who attacked you."

He turned and walked out of her room without waiting for a reply. When he was gone, Cecilia pressed her burning cheeks against the cold wall.

"He wants me to give him an answer about how I feel about him... What do I do now?"

It was the afternoon of the following day, the second day of the Week of Ashes. It was Eins' turn to ride with Lean, but he swapped with Cecilia, since he'd taken over from her the other day. The parade ended without incident. Now, Cecilia was walking with Lean down the streets. Cecilia was still in the black military uniform, but Lean had changed out of her parade outfit into a black dress. She was explaining to Cecilia about Advent traditions, pointing upward with her index finger.

"The Week of Ashes represents the times when demons ruled the land. Before Advent merged with the harvest festival, this was a time to practice modesty and frugality."

"Really?"

"It used to be customary to fast and give up smoking during this period. The point of giving up all sorts of pleasures was to imagine how awful life had been and feel even more gratitude for the goddess who freed people from suffering."

"Hmm."

"But this changed when the harvest festival became incorporated into Advent. Now the Week of Ashes is only about appearances, and the Week of Light has become more extravagant. I hear that a costume ball is the highlight for the nobility nowadays!"

"Huh!"

"You're not really listening, are you?"

"What?"

Lean stopped pointing and scrutinized her friend's face. She had sussed out that something had happened. Cecilia took a step back with a start, as if to escape Lean's piercing gaze.

"It-it's nothing, honestly!"

"I *thought* you seemed spaced out when we were riding in the carriage."

"No, I wasn't! Maybe it looked that way to you because I was feeling tired?"

"Really?"

Cecilia couldn't meet Lean's eyes. Though she was her good friend, she didn't want to admit even to her that the thing that had been on her mind, keeping her distracted, was Oscar's confession and her own lack of an answer to it. This was partially down to her own embarrassment, but she also thought that this should stay between her and Oscar.

Since their last conversation, Cecilia had been thinking so hard about what she should do that she could barely eat. Nagging questions kept her awake at night, and she kept spacing out during the day. Yet despite all this earnest thinking, she still couldn't decide what to say to Oscar.

I appreciate Lean's concern, but this is a problem I should solve on my own...

"Let me guess, someone told you they have feelings for you?"

Bam! Cecilia crashed into a stone pillar. She stared at Lean in utter shock. Her friend crossed her arms, grinning at how she'd read Cecilia like an open book.

"Y-yes, but how did you...?"

"Well, well, you admitted it right away. I'm surprised he didn't get rid of the obstacles in the way first before confessing to you."

"What obstacles?"

Cecilia was so lost. The way Lean was talking, it seemed she was aware of Oscar's feelings. But Cecilia had never told her that he'd confessed his love for her some time ago when they met in the academy infirmary.

"Lean, you knew about him?"

"It was obvious."

"Was it?"

"Anyone with eyes could see it! The biggest mystery was how you didn't!"

"Oh…"

Cecilia looked down, embarrassed. She really had no idea Oscar had fallen in love with her right until he'd told her in no uncertain terms, despite the fact she'd learned it was apparent to everyone else. She used to think Oscar was a bit dim for not having realized Cecil's true identity, but it turned out that she was the clueless one…

Lean seemed relieved that she could finally talk about this openly.

"I didn't expect him to confess to you so soon, though. I never took Gilbert for the impatient type."

"What?"

"Huh?"

Cecilia tilted her head, not understanding.

"What has Gilbert got to do with it?"

"What do you mean? We were talking about how he's confessed his love for you?"

And at that moment, time seemed to stop, and Cecilia forgot to breathe. She slowly dropped her gaze and stood still for three whole minutes before staring up at the sky, her head tilted to the side.

"Can you say that again?"

"We were talking about Gilbert's love confession."

"You've got to be kidding me!"

Passersby turned to look as Cecilia screamed at the top of her lungs, but they quickly lost interest, assuming the two were a couple having a spat in public.

"Where's this coming from? About Gilbert?"

"Oh. So it wasn't him?"

"N-no, of course not! It was Oscar!"

"Really, he was first?"

"First?"

Cecilia pressed her fingers to her temples. Gilbert's name coming up out of nowhere had given her a headache.

"Why are you bringing up my brother?"

"Do you even need to ask?"

"I...do?"

"He loves you. As a girl."

Shocking revelations can cause your mind to go blank. Cecilia found that out for the first time at that moment.

"Jade and Doctor Mordred may not know that you're a girl, but don't forget there are others who do. I'm sure Dante and Grace know!"

"You can't be serious! Gilbert sees me as nothing more than a sister!"

Cecilia lowered her voice so as not to be overheard, but her next statement was tinged with intense emotion.

"*Adoptive* sister! Strictly speaking, you're a not-too-closely-related girl he's sharing a roof with!"

"That's not untrue, but..."

She couldn't admit that Gilbert could see her as a romantic interest. She was engaged and would one day become queen, while he would go on to head a powerful noble house that supported her. Their various responsibilities had kept them so busy since early childhood that she struggled to remember the times they'd even gotten to play together.

"Besides, hasn't Gilbert made your heart swoon at least a few times?"

"Uh..."

Cecilia conspicuously averted her gaze. Lean smiled triumphantly.

"You can't fool me! I know in your past life that Gilbert was your top choice in the game!"

Cecilia couldn't respond at first, but eventually, blushing fervently, she admitted:

"You're right about that… But I'm not like you, Lean."

"What are you trying to say?"

"You crush on your favorite characters, but I don't."

"Then why was he your favorite?"

Lean couldn't conceive of another reason to like a character in a dating sim.

"Because Gilbert was, like, the second most pitiful character in the game after Cecilia."

In *Holy Maiden of Vleugel Academy 3*, Gilbert is a recluse, traumatized by an unhappy childhood. Due to his antisocial nature, he only appears in his own scenario. This meant that outside his route, he never recovers from his trauma to find happiness.

"I wanted for him to be happy with Lean in the game. It's not viable in this world, of course, not with you being the heroine."

"I'm not any worse than the game Lean!"

She narrowed her eyes, mildly upset about Cecilia's rudeness.

"So you romanced him in the game purely out of kindness?"

"That's right."

"You sure?"

"Yes!"

Cecilia pouted at her friend's accusations. The truth was, however, that Gilbert *had* sent her heart racing on more than one occasion. She was really into his scenario in the game, and in this world, she'd reacted strongly when he took off her shirt to check her bruise and when he'd called her "dear."

Hold on, why am I taking what she's saying for a fact?

Now that she'd recovered from shock, the gears in Cecilia's brain were turning yet again. Lean could be wrong about Gilbert. His kindness toward her was nothing more than brotherly love for his hopeless sister. It wasn't romantic love—no way.

After she calmed down, Lean patted her on the back.

"Anyway, let's live our new lives to the fullest!"

"I think you're taking that a bit too far in your case…"

"You say that, but wouldn't you be sad for me if I held back from unleashing my full potential?"

Cecilia's friend from her past life knew her through and through. Though she was often reluctant to participate in Lean's pet projects, Cecilia would have hated it if Lean couldn't do what she enjoyed because she was too shy to ask for help.

"I guess I would," she acquiesced with a smile.

"I love that about you," Lean said, smiling back at her.

"Do you have anything planned for later?"

They were sitting on a café terrace where they'd had a late lunch. Lean paused, her fork poised to stab at a slice of chiffon cake, and a cute smile appeared on her lips.

"I sure do! I'm going on a date with Huey!"

"You really are living your life to the fullest, huh?"

"I am, and you should, too!"

Lean giggled and brought a piece of cake to her mouth. She touched her fingertips to her cheek as she was chewing, delighted with the taste. She was in a terribly good mood today.

Cecilia took a sip of her tea.

"And what about you, Cecilia? It's a big day for you. Why didn't your folks come to see you? Are they not interested?"

"Come on, there's no way I'd invite them! And if they turned up by some fluke, I definitely wouldn't talk to them!"

"Why?"

"Because of this?"

She gestured at her outfit. Lean made big eyes at her.

"No way… You didn't tell your parents you're dressing as a boy?"

"Nope. Seriously, why did you think I'd tell them? They may be forgiving, but they'd never approve of me pretending to be a boy at the academy!"

"How did you manage to keep it secret from them?"

"I just didn't tell them?"

Cecilia tilted her head and Lean mirrored her.

"But shouldn't the duke's network of informants have picked up on it?"

"Oh, if it isn't Miss Lean!"

They turned when they heard a familiar voice. A lady with honey-blond hair just like Cecilia's and a gentleman with sapphire eyes, also exactly like Cecilia's, entered the terrace. A knight looking after their safety followed behind them.

Mom, Dad, and Hans?!

Speak of the devil. Cecilia's parents had thought to visit the café just as she was there. She stifled a scream and turned her face away from them. They didn't seem to have noticed her as they approached Lean.

"It's good to see you, Your Grace."

Lean stood up and curtsied to Lucinda Sylvie, who smiled at her benevolently. Cecilia's father came closer.

"It's a pleasure to meet you, Miss Lean. My name is Edward Sylvie. I hear you're a good friend of our daughter."

"It's an honor to meet you as well, Your Grace. You have a wonderful daughter."

Lean curtsied, smiling gently. The air about her changed dramatically as she played a polite, well-brought up young lady. Hearing her talk about Cecilia with respect and admiration felt new.

"Are you enjoying a day out about town? Taking part in the festivities?"

"We are now that we've escaped from Gilbert."

"Sorry?"

Lean didn't understand. Lucinda Sylvie smiled and clarified her husband's enigmatic remark.

"Gilbert offered to take us around and show us the sights, but he wouldn't let us explore freely. Don't go there, that road is dangerous, blah-blah. So we snuck away."

"We've got Hans with us for protection. Gilbert is such a worrywart, bless his soul."

Edward Sylvie guffawed, and Lucinda smiled. Lean whispered to Cecilia without looking at her:

"I can totally tell that these guys are your parents."

"I-I'm not that naive!"

"Really? I think you're birds of a feather," Lean snapped. "I'll distract them while you make your getaway. I'm assuming you don't want them to learn your secret?"

"You'll do that for me, Lean? Thanks!"

"I like having you in my debt."

Lean's motivation unsettled Cecilia, but she felt immensely grateful to her at that moment, nonetheless. When she saw out of the corner of her eye that Lean had engaged her parents in conversation, she lightly stood up from her chair. Just as she was about to make a stealthy retreat, her eyes met those of Hans, who had been standing by out of the way.

"Were you leaving?"

"Um..."

"Excuse me, but do I know your name?"

Her sneaky attempt to exit must have caught his attention. Not having recognized her, Hans stared at her coldly. Normally he'd greet her with a pleasant smile and a "How's your day going, Miss?" or "Fair warning, your next sword practice will be a serious workout!" but he behaved very differently toward suspicious strangers, as she found out.

She quickly turned away from him, desperately trying to hide her face, but that backfired—now she was facing Edward and Lucinda.

Oh, crap...

She hung her head, but it was too late. Her parents noticed her with surprise and exchanged glances.

"Isn't that…?"

"Er… I'm just…"

"Cecilia, darling!"

Nooooo!

She broke out in a cold sweat, blinking nervously as she found herself in what felt not just like a pickle, but a whole jar of them.

This isn't going to end well for me…

She was going to be dragged back home by her parents; they'd be furious at her for dressing up as a boy. She'd be exposed as a Holy Maiden candidate and be forced to attend the academy as a girl, which would trigger the Bad Ending—her death sentence.

This future scenario unfolding in her head terrified her so much that the world started spinning.

I have to fool them somehow!

She raised her head, frantically thinking of what she could do…

"You look absolutely fantastic, darling! That's my daughter, dashing in whatever she wears!"

"Hearing about it from Gilbert is one thing, but seeing you dressed like this in person is another. This style really suits you, Cecilia!"

"Whuh?"

Cecilia froze, thrown by their unexpected reaction. She noticed that Lean also had an unnatural expression on her face.

"Wait… Gil told you about this?"

"Oops. We weren't supposed to tell you, were we?"

"I think that's what he tried to impress on us, yes. But he's not here, so I don't see a problem…"

Cecilia's dad roared with laughter and her mom giggled. Only Hans was shocked, exclaiming, "M-Miss Cecilia?! Wh-why are you dressed like this?!"

What's going on…?

She honestly had no clue. But just as she was about to cry from confusion, she heard the voice she missed the most at that moment.

"I looked for you everywhere. What are you doing here, of all places...? Oh."

Gilbert squeezed through the crowd of customers. He jerked to a halt when he saw that his parents were with Cecilia and uttered a long groan that was very much out of character for him.

"Gil, can you explain this to me?" Cecilia asked shakily.

Her brother covered his face, fingertips touching his forehead. "All right..."

"There's no rule about using your real name to enroll at Vleugel Academy, nor is it a requirement for girls to wear girls' uniforms," Gilbert began.

He was sitting in the chair Lean had been using before, opposite the very confused Cecilia. Their parents, Lean, and even Hans had already left. Lean had her date, and the others went to see the sights.

"I know that. They never specified those things because they took it for granted that everyone would use their real name. And before I showed up, they didn't have any cases of students wanting to wear uniforms designed for the other gender."

Before enrolling at the academy, she asked Gilbert many times to check the rules in case people found out she was a girl. Her line of defense would be that it didn't say anywhere she couldn't dress like a boy.

"Right. But although what you're doing isn't explicitly forbidden, the academy's supervisor, Count Clemence, would certainly have an issue with it."

"Why?"

"Because it's preposterous for a duke's daughter to attend his prestigious institution under a false identity and pretend to be a boy on top of that. Since he's a man of high rank, he could report it to the king, in addition to House Sylvie."

"But he hasn't reported me to the king, right?"

"He hasn't, because I silenced him using both influence and money."

Cecilia needed a moment to process the shocking information he'd just delivered in a perfectly nonchalant tone.

Gilbert continued, watching his dumbfounded sister out of the corner of one eye.

"It's not exactly a closely guarded secret that Count Clemence's heir has a gambling addiction. From that, I surmised his house was strapped for cash. I offered to provide the count with cash in return for his silence. But obviously, I don't have a private fund from which to take the money out..."

"I see. So you explained the situation to Mom and Dad and got them to pay off the count?"

"That's right. Our parents were considering donating money to the academy to begin with, for as long as we were students there. What I did was ask them to make the funding dependent on certain conditions."

Until someone asks, don't mention that our daughter is attending the academy dressed as a boy.

Arrange it so that Cecilia will be able to lead a normal life at the academy while passing for a boy.

If the king asked whether it was true that Cecilia was studying at the academy as a male student, the count was free to answer in the affirmative and even disclose the conditions specified by House Sylvie. He would not be held accountable for anything.

The count would receive a handsome amount of money at regular intervals for turning a blind eye to Cecilia's harmless antics. It was a deal almost too good to be true, so he accepted it without a second thought.

"Since our parents are good friends with the king, he probably assumed he'd be pardoned for keeping that secret, even in the worst-case scenario."

Cecilia lurched forward.

"W-wait a moment, what exactly did you tell Mom and Dad? You said you explained the situation. Did you tell them about my past life?!"

"Don't be silly. I told them you wanted to enroll using a fake identity to broaden your horizons."

"Huh... And they believed that?"

"Yup. It even moved Mom to tears. 'She's finally serious about preparing for her future role as the queen,' she said. Dad also agreed that broad horizons are a must for being a good co-ruler of the country and insisted he wouldn't be stingy."

"Mom... Dad..."

Her parents had always doted on her, but she hadn't expected them to be so supportive of her follies. In the game, her parents' uncritical, boundless affection toward their daughter turned Cecilia into a mean, selfish girl. This time around, however, things were different.

Cecilia leaned back in the chair, relieved.

"I wish you'd told me sooner! I'd have been more relaxed about this whole—"

"Which is precisely why I didn't tell you."

"Huh?"

"If you'd known from the start you had the backing of House Sylvie, you'd have thrown caution to the wind. Am I wrong? I didn't tell you because you'd get in so much trouble even I wouldn't be able to save you."

He sounded exasperated when he said that. Cecilia shrank back and squeaked out an apologetic "You're right..." His assessment was absolutely correct.

Gilbert sighed with resignation and looked at the cup in his hand.

"There's no changing the fact you've found out about it, but please act like you can't count on our parents' support. Remember that it's not you, my dear Cecilia, who will bear the brunt of responsibility for any mishaps."

"Um, Gil?"

He looked up from his drink at her, but she dropped her gaze to avoid his.

"There's something I wanted to ask you, but it's on a different topic…"

"Shoot."

"What's up with 'dear Cecilia'?"

She was a bit nervous asking him about that. He'd stopped calling her "sis" recently and instead was going with "dear Cecilia." It made her wonder if he saw her in a different light than before, but she'd felt too anxious to bring it up earlier.

"You don't like it?"

"I don't hate it, but I kind of miss you calling me 'sis.'"

"Well, we're not really siblings, though."

He smiled awkwardly. That reminded Cecilia of what Lean had told her earlier that day.

"He loves you. As a girl."

"Strictly speaking, you're a not-too-closely-related girl he's sharing a roof with!"

He doesn't feel like we're siblings because I'm so unlike him; I'm not resourceful or confident…

But no matter how much she tried to convince herself of that line of thinking, Lean's words kept haunting Cecilia. It was ludicrous to suggest Gilbert loved her in that way—but somehow her neck started feeling hot, and heat rose to her face. She had the unbearable sensation of dryness in her mouth.

"What's the matter?"

"Wh-why, what matter?!"

"You're looking strangely uncomfortable."

He reached his hand to her cheek. She drew her body back reflexively, and then he pinched her.

"Ha-ha, you should see your face!"

"Argh…"

Normally she wouldn't have though much of this sort of teasing, but Lean's love theory made her self-conscious, so she tensed up.

"Seriously, though, what's wrong? Are you feeling sick?"

"N-no, it's nothing…"

"Do you have a fever?"

Gilbert stood up and walked over to check her temperature. She felt his cool hand first on her forehead, and then on the side of her neck, from which a scorching heat was radiating from.

Eek!

This wasn't anything out of the ordinary. Being this close was perfectly normal for family…

"You're a little warm," Gilbert said, his attitude neutral.

Cecilia clenched her fists resting on her knees.

I-I've got to pull myself together! It's not fair to Gil, and I hate feeling so self-conscious around him…

It was just wrong for her to react as if Gilbert had romantic intentions for her. She stood up abruptly.

Honesty is always the best!

"Gil!"

"Yes?"

"Lean said something weird to me earlier today…"

She needed to hear Gilbert deny that what Lean had said was true, to confirm that their relationship was purely that of step-siblings, wholesome and sweet. That's why she decided to tell Gilbert about it.

"She said that you love me…"

For a second, Gilbert froze in surprise. But he quickly got over it and smiled uncertainly.

"And? Why would that be weird? I've been telling you that I love you."

"You misunderstand, she didn't mean it like that. She thinks you love me in a romantic way…"

Wait…

Now that she got that off her chest, her head cooled down, and she could think clearly again. Cecilia reflected on what she'd said.

Did I just…make an absolute fool of myself?!

She broke out in a cold sweat again as her breath grew hot and her hands started shaking. Lean's theory was so stupid that she'd actually repeated it to Gilbert as if she believed it?! She shut her eyes, too scared to see Gilbert's reaction.

"S-sorry! That was so dumb! Please just forget about it… It's not that I doubt you…"

"Why are you getting worked up about it now, of all times?"

Cecilia glanced at him timorously when he interrupted her. Gilbert was smiling faintly, his gaze firmly fixed on his cup of coffee. He might have been staring at his own reflection.

"I've always used the word 'love' toward you in a romantic way, you know."

He looked up, and his eyes met hers.

"I love you, my dear Cecilia."

He smiled with his eyes, blushing. That delicate pink tint to his cheeks overloaded Cecilia's brain for the day. She felt fit to burst.

In the world of Cecilia's past life, it was said that "love comes banging at the door three times in a lifetime." But now it was like she was getting two lifetime's worth of romantic attention all at once.

* * *

Dear goddess, call it off. This isn't the time...

Three days had passed since the shocking love confession from Gilbert. It was now the fifth day of the Week of Ashes.

Cecilia was sitting with her head in her hands outside the orphanage, where she had come for a rehearsal. The dilemma that was giving her a headache was, of course, the matter of Gilbert's and Oscar's love for her.

They both seemed okay with giving me as much time as I needed to give them a reply, but I can't delay it indefinitely! That said, I can't give either of them an answer I'm not sure of myself. That would be inconsiderate...

She cared for them so much, so she had to carefully consider her feelings toward them with honesty. The problem was that she had zero experience with love outside of games. The experience of having received two passionate confessions threw her into a state of confusion, tormenting her day and night.

I'm so fed up with this...

Faint rings were forming under her eyes from lack of sleep.

"Cecil, are you okay?"

She lifted her head to face Eins, who had come up to her. He seemed worried.

"I saw you at the rehearsal. The show is just around the corner, but you kept flubbing your lines?"

"Yeah, well... I've got a lot going on in my private life lately..."

"More of the nasties?"

"What nasties?"

"People dropping flowerpots or buckets of hot water on you or throwing eggs?"

"Ah, I'd forgotten about that."

The bombshell love confessions made her forget all about the bullying. She had a lot on her plate, with the guys proclaiming their love to her all of a sudden, the rehearsals, searching for the bully, and trying to complete the twins' route. She wasn't at capacity—she was over it.

Maybe I should speak with Grace again about the twins?

She would probably be more willing to tell her more now that Cecilia had already learned about their past.

I'll go and see her after we're done with the play.

The production would be shown over five days: the last two days of the Week of Ashes, Advent Day on October 31, and the first two days of the Week of Light. Some of the city theaters were already showing their Advent plays, but Lean's production had very limited funding—just proceeds from her book sales and donations from House Machias. She'd chosen the five days in the middle of the festival period, when celebrations were in full swing, to attract the biggest audience.

In other words, the premiere was tomorrow.

"I bet it's all very taxing on you. Why don't you go for a walk and see if it clears your head? You still have plenty of break time left."

"That's an idea. I guess I'll do that."

She had to pull herself together, for the sake of the hardworking theater troupe if nothing else. A stroll and a bit of a change of scenery might indeed help. She got up, and to her surprise, Eins stood beside her.

"I can't leave you on your own, or something might happen again. Besides, I feel like going for a walk myself."

His concern wasn't unwelcome. They left the orphanage grounds together.

The area around the orphanage wasn't as crowded as the city center, but it was busy nonetheless. There were lots of street stalls selling freshly grilled meats or fruit liquors, while green spaces were occupied by groups of children sitting down for story time.

The picture books the storytellers were reading from were based on the legend of the goddess fighting off the demons.

Cecilia was amazed at the sight.

"Wow…"

"Huh? Don't tell me you've never been here before?"

"I have, but I've never had the chance to take a proper look at everything that's going on here. I thought there wasn't much to see in the city outside of the center."

Cecilia glanced around curiously as Eins watched her, amused.

"It is the biggest festival of the year, remember? People even come from abroad to see it."

"Right!"

Advent celebrations were held in her home region as well, of course, but they couldn't compare to the festival in the capital. Advent Day was celebrated with pomp where she'd grown up, but the Weeks of Ashes and Light weren't anything special.

"Hmm? The people over there are dressed normally."

Cecilia was looking at a group of men standing together. There were four, no, five of them, all wearing ordinary clothes, with red handkerchiefs in their breast pockets.

"Those guys? That's because they're in the Caritade counter-movement."

"Counter-movement?"

Cecilia tilted her neck, awaiting an explanation.

"I talked before about the north of the country being extremely religious, remember? It's the opposite for here in the south, where Caritade believers are rare. The non-believers wear their usual attire with something red during the festive period."

"Ah…"

"In some regions, the goddess is actually considered to be one of the demons. People from those parts oppose the Church of Caritade for that reason."

"You know so much, Eins!"

"After everything happened to Zwei and me, we decided to educate ourselves on the topic."

Cecilia assumed he was alluding to their mother being murdered by a religious fanatic.

"And what we learned was that all those people have one thing in common: their beliefs are founded upon made-up stories. Devils coming in twins, the goddess actually being a demon...the entire origin myth is just a story people take as fact."

"Wait, even the legend of the Holy Maiden?"

"Yeah. There's a presence in this land that makes people go crazy, and some people have the power to stop it—that much is true. But the rest is just a tale someone invented to explain why things are the way they are."

Eins smiled wryly and added in an ironic tone:

"I never imagined that Zwei and I would become part of that story one day, though."

Cecilia studied his expression as they walked.

"You'd better watch where you're going, or you'll trip on something."

"Uh, right... Yikes!"

Just as she turned her head, she bumped into a person coming from the opposite direction. The impact made her fall on her butt.

"Are you okay?!"

"Are you all right?!"

Eins and the other person called out in unison. Cecilia looked up, meeting the eyes of a man in an ashen robe. His irises were purple, like amethysts. The man had beige hair and slender limbs. He was also surprisingly handsome.

"I'm so sorry, I was distracted and didn't see you coming."

He smiled and helped her up. Cecilia noticed that he had a companion standing behind him. The other man had long black hair and was wearing glasses. He seemed to be staring at Cecilia with outright hostility—either that, or his gaze was naturally pointed.

Wait... Have I seen these guys before?

She blinked a few times. She couldn't remember meeting them, yet they seemed familiar. A sense of déjà vu like that could only mean...

They're characters from the game?

Still, try as she might, Cecilia couldn't remember any characters with eyes and hair that color.

Maybe they were just background characters? Though I could be wrong about this.

The man who helped her to her feet didn't let go of her hand. He scrutinized her.

"Forgive me if I'm mistaken, but aren't you one of the Holy Maiden's knights?"

"Oh, how did you know?"

Cecilia widened her eyes in surprise. She wasn't wearing her dress uniform from the other day, just a black shirt and slacks.

Reassured that he wasn't confusing her for someone else, the man explained:

"I saw you at the parade. Were you okay after getting hit with that egg?"

"Uh, yeah, it didn't hurt me."

So it wasn't when she swapped turns with Eins that he'd seen her, but the day before that.

The man squeezed her hand with both of his, a look of concern on his face.

"There are some horrible people out there. They were probably just jealous of all the attention you were getting."

He smiled at her warmly, looking more charming at that moment than some of the love interests from the game. Cecilia's cheeks took on a slightly pinkish hue.

"Oh, sorry, I've been thoughtless. I didn't mean to hold you up here. But it was a pleasure to meet you. I hope our paths will cross again sometime."

He finally let go of Cecilia's hand, said "Good-bye!" and left with his companion. Cecilia idly watched them walk away, lost in thought. That's when she realized that Eins had been oddly quiet. She turned to him and saw that he, too, was still staring in the direction where the two guys had disappeared.

"What's the matter, Eins?"

"I think I've seen that man before."

"Really?"

"In Cuddy's house... I don't know, maybe he just looked similar."

Sometimes, seeing a particular person can ruin your whole morning.

"Good morning!"

"Good morning..."

It was the sixth day of the Week of Ashes. Lean ambushed Gilbert the moment he stepped out of the dorm. She was dressed in her school uniform. Gilbert reluctantly muttered a greeting, wishing he didn't have to deal with her at all that day. Completely unfazed by his attitude, Lean beamed back at him.

"I have a present for you, Lord Gilbert."

"A present?"

"I've been saving it for you!"

Perhaps because they were in public, Lean was using a saccharine tone. She trotted over to him, acting cute and girly. Other students passing by shot them curious glances, surprised to see them together. Gilbert held his hand out to stop her from invading his personal space.

"Thanks, but I don't really want a present from you."

"Oh, don't say that before you know what it is!"

She took hold of Gilbert's hand and pressed a piece of paper into it. He unwillingly unfolded it.

"What's this? A ticket to a play?"

"It's my special gift for you! Well, I say special, but I've been giving them out for free anyway," she replied with a big smile.

Hearing the tickets were free, Gilbert thought at first that they were for some trashy show and that she was forcing him to take it just to make him waste his time. Then he noticed the name of the play's director and producer on the ticket: Madame Neal. This appeared to be part of some new nefarious scheme of hers.

"You don't have to come if you don't want to see it, but you WILL regret missing out."

"Why?"

"My apologies, but I have to get going! I must deliver a ticket to Lord Oscar, too."

Lean quickly stepped away from Gilbert and turned to go with a flourish of her skirt. She looked back at him with a daring smile as she bid him farewell.

So the prince is also invited, and I'd supposedly regret not going?

Cecilia's face flashed in his mind. There was no doubt she was somehow involved in this.

"She's been acting secretive lately... What on earth did she get wrapped up in this time?"

Gilbert heaved a sigh, deflating at the thought of his dearest, naive Cecilia falling victim to yet another of Lean's ploys.

That evening, ticket in hand, Gilbert made a trip to a place he'd normally be highly unlikely to visit—the Cigogne Orphanage, where, according to the information on the ticket, the play would be shown.

The large open area outside the orphanage building, which was usually occupied by children playing, now featured a fine wooden stage. There were no numbered seats—instead, the spectators were free to choose a place to sit anywhere on the simple wooden benches arranged in front of the stage. To the side were stalls selling refreshments, pamphlets with the script and a list of the actors, and for some reason, Lean's books. On closer inspection, the cover was different from what Gilbert had seen before, so it seemed to be a new publication.

Gilbert had already noticed a familiar redhead sitting on one of the benches when he was presenting his ticket at the gate. The other guests had given him a wide berth, no doubt too intimidated to sit close to a royal. Gilbert approached him from behind.

"I see you're tempting fate, Your Highness, coming here without your escort."

"Well, if it isn't Gilbert."

Oscar looked up as the boy sat down next to him.

"Your bodyguards must be a pain to drag around wherever you go, but you are our king-to-be. What if something happened to you?"

"You can worry about that if something happens. I have my younger brothers, so one of them will take my place if need be."

"This again…"

"Each of them is more than capable of ruling our country, I assure you," Oscar said dispassionately, as if the matter didn't matter to him one bit.

Gilbert sighed. It wasn't the future of the country he was worried about, but Oscar himself. Not that he'd ever admit to it aloud.

When Gilbert had gone quiet, Oscar fished out a slip of paper from his pocket.

"Did you get one from Lean, too?"

"Indeed. Watching a play tonight wasn't in my plans, but I changed my mind when I learned Cecil was in it."

"He's in the play?!"

"Did you not realize?"

Gilbert stared at him, baffled. Whenever Oscar failed to notice something glaringly obvious, he wondered whether he'd really be okay when he took over as the king. He was a very accomplished young man, that much was certain, but his wits could use some sharpening.

"Then why did you come? Didn't you have anything better to do?"

"I felt obliged to, since it's for charity. And besides, I wanted to take a look at how the orphanage is run for myself."

"The church is in charge of that, though. Even if you had any objections to how they manage it, this is entirely out of your sphere of influence."

"That's all the more reason for me to check it out."

Gilbert stared at him with more attention.

"It's the duty of the government to look after the welfare of its citizens, and the orphans housed here are our citizens. It may take some time to effect change, but eventually, I would like the state to handle caring for them," Oscar elaborated, his gaze fixed on the stage. "I envisage this as a joint project between the royal government and the church."

Gilbert's intense gaze must have finally gotten to Oscar, who turned to face him.

"What is it?"

"Nothing. What you said changed the way I was thinking about something, but don't worry about it."

"I won't then." Oscar let it go, returning his gaze to the stage. People were milling around to the left and right. The curtain would be up shortly.

"By the way, I've been meaning to ask you..."

"Yes?" Gilbert glanced at Oscar quizzically, surprised by the serious tone of his voice.

"What are your feelings for Cecilia?"

"...You don't beat around the bush."

"I believe it's best to be direct in cases like this."

The theater crew seemed to have finished their preparations, and an actress from Gleick's Theater Company serving as the narrator took to the stage. Gilbert had his eyes on the curtain rising behind her when he answered Oscar's question.

"Let me just say that your suspicions are correct."

"I see. So I have a rival. I'd better not underestimate you."

"I could say the same for you."

At that moment, Cecilia emerged from the wings. She was wearing a platinum-silver wig with straight hair unlike her naturally curly locks and a pure white dress that gave her an air of holiness. While the color of her eyes was unchanged, their beauty was even more striking, accentuated by the elaborate makeup.

"My fiancée isn't just cute; she's beautiful...," Oscar muttered incomprehensibly to Gilbert, who kept his eyes on the stage.

In the first scene, the goddess laments that demons rule the land. The story followed Prosper Kingdom's legend, but Lean added some lines and scenes to present it in a more dramatic way.

Next was the battle between the goddess and the demons. The skirt of Cecilia's dress featured long slits, presumably for ease of movement, but also to allow glimpses of her bare legs underneath, eliciting noises of admiration from some of the male members of the audience.

"Tsk!"

Gilbert smacked his tongue in annoyance. The play wasn't vulgar, but he'd nonetheless make sure to complain afterward to Lean about the outfit she made Cecilia wear. She should sew in a second layer of fabric under those slits for the next performances.

Those were the thoughts running through his head as he silenced the excitable guys sitting behind him with a death glare.

"The play is put together surprisingly well. I had been slightly

apprehensive about it suddenly morphing into a steamy gay romance, on account of Lean being the producer."

"She probably didn't want to risk upsetting the clergy. Don't forget she was raised here," Gilbert replied.

Lean was certainly concealing her true intentions, but she did care about the orphanage, too. At least that's what Gilbert presumed based on the fact that the refreshment and pamphlet stalls were staffed by the children who lived there. The proceeds would directly support the institution.

Meanwhile, the play was reaching its climax. The final part of the legend was the most famous. In a vicious attack, the demons cast the goddess down into infernal flames. Then a man came to her rescue. Pretty much all of the plays based on the legend ended there, with the narrator's closing line being, "A child was born to the goddess and the man who had assisted her. The man became the first king of our nation."

Both Gilbert and Oscar had seen performances of this tale many times. Thus far, Lean's version wasn't novel in any way besides her unusual choice for the lead actor.

Orange light mimicking flames shined onto Cecilia, who raised her hand in a plea for help. A young man came to her aid. Now it was the narrator's turn... Except that they stayed silent.

Normally the curtain would fall after this scene, but it stayed aloft. The goddess and the young man stood at the center of the stage, facing each other.

"I am so glad that you are safe, my goddess."
"But why would you risk your life for my sake?"
"I could not have done otherwise, for I have fallen in love with you."

The sugary lines made a vein pop out on Gilbert's temple. Oscar, too, seemed unsure about this romantic development.

* * *

"My heart has been your prisoner ever since the night you descended to Earth and took on human form."

"In my brief time among humans, I've relied on you more than anyone, for which I am grateful."

"My goddess, you have accomplished what you had set out to do here on Earth. But I cannot bear to part with you, never to see you again, wondering if you have been but a dream."

"I also wish to stay with you…"

The orchestra stopped playing, and the two actors stood unnaturally close to each other. The man put his hands on Cecilia's hips, brought her close, and leaned in to place his lips over hers…

"NO!"

"Stop!"

Gilbert and Oscar stood up simultaneously, earning mortified glares from the other audience members. The curtain dropped before the actors' lips met, and applause followed. Oscar and Gilbert went over to the wing of the stage while the rest of the audience was still clapping.

"You guys were amazing! Thanks to you, my books are selling like hotcakes!"

When Gilbert and Oscar burst into the backstage room, they were greeted by Lean, who seemed to be in the very best of moods.

She basically told them that the novels she was selling were the second volume of her gay romance story, whose characters were modeled on Cecil and Oscar. In one of the scenes in the book, Oran and Crow jump to their feet when they see Cecil being kissed in a play. She'd invited Gilbert and Oscar to see it to have them unknowingly re-enact that part.

Needless to say, Crow was based on Gilbert. He got his name-sake from Gilbert's black hair.

"I was distributing tickets along with that chapter from my story to everyone but you. I expect that the people who came to see the play after reading it might think it's not just fiction after your stunt! Their minds will go straight to the gutter every time they see you from now on! That's how I make fellow perverts out of unsuspecting citizens!"

Oscar, standing next to Gilbert, furrowed his brow.

"So essentially, you used us?"

"Me, using Your Highness? Oh no, no! It just so happened that your feelings were in tune with the characters in my book, and you inadvertently acted just like them, incidentally, for my benefit!"

Her bright, contagious smile had no effect on Oscar, who grasped his head in vexation.

"I'm ashamed to admit that I have the urge to hit a girl for the first time in my life."

"Oddly enough, I feel exactly the same," said Gilbert, a sour look on his face.

Lean raised her hands.

"Now, now, let's stay calm! Lord Cecil didn't actually get kissed, and besides, the other character was being played by a woman!"

"What, that wasn't a man?"

"I knew that scene would make you especially mad if it was a man, so I had an actress perform that role. My life is very dear to me, you know?"

It was only now that Gilbert noticed a woman lying down on a rush mat behind Lean. She might have been the actress who'd played the man who falls for the goddess. At least that was Gilbert's best guess, based on how she was so flushed that she was practically steaming while muttering "He has such a pretty face…" in delirium.

Zwei was tending to the actress, while Eins scolded her.

"Isn't it time you built up some resistance?"

"I thought you two might come."

Gilbert and Oscar turned at once, hearing Cecilia's voice. She hadn't had the time to change out of her goddess costume yet.

"I saw you in the audience, so I guessed you might want to come and see me after the show," Cecilia said a bit bashfully.

"It was a good performance," said Oscar.

"Thanks…" Cecilia smiled shyly.

Seeing Cecilia's outfit, Gilbert suddenly remembered the complaint he intended to make. He looked up to glare at Lean.

"I almost forgot. Lean, you have to do something about those thigh slits."

"Thigh slits?" asked Oscar. Apparently, he'd failed to notice them.

"Oh, these?"

Cecilia pinched the side of the skirt and fluttered it. It only took the sight of her bare kneecap to make Oscar shudder.

"What?! You wore this on stage in front of people?!"

"Um, yes? Do you think it looks silly on me?"

"Just…just don't shake it like that! Y-you'll catch a cold!"

Oscar took his coat off and put it over her shoulders. It did nothing to cover her legs, but he wasn't thinking rationally at that moment. Gilbert pointed to Oscar with his thumb.

"A lot of guys had a similar reaction during the play. Add another layer of fabric under the skirt, or I may have to kill the leering crowd next time."

"Indeed, this outfit needs to be fixed," Oscar agreed.

Neither expected Lean to concede without putting up a fight, but she did. Except that she tacked on her own conditions.

"Sure, and you'll be helping with the play from tomorrow on!"

"What?"

"Where's this coming from now?"

The two guys looked at Lean in bewilderment. She put her hand to her chest, making a serious face.

"I'm terribly short-handed here. Both me and the rest of the crew are barely coping at the moment. We need all the help we can get."

"That's none of our concern…"

Lean smiled sadly upon hearing this blunt rejection.

"Ah, well… In that case, the alterations to Lord Cecil's stage costume will have to be put on hold, I'm afraid."

"You don't mean it!"

"Oh, but I do. I have so much work to do I don't even sleep at night! I make repairs to costumes damaged during rehearsals and keep tweaking the script! So I really have no time to be making changes to a costume that is completely fine in my eyes!"

Oscar and Gilbert fell silent, not knowing how to respond.

"But if you agree to help out, that might free up some of my time for the alterations. Well? Will you do it?"

Gilbert and Oscar exchanged looks. After a brief pause, they both nodded.

"Thank you so much!" Lean chirped.

It was the last day of the Week of Ashes, when the second show would be held.

"These rehearsals are killing me!"

Cecilia slumped down onto a chair in a room the orphanage was letting them use as a dressing room. She had it all to herself, so as not to give anyone a chance to find out that she was really a girl.

There was still some time before that day's show, so she wasn't wearing her stage getup yet.

"Now we even have people turning up to watch our rehearsals. I already feel more tired than after yesterday's performance...," she grumbled, staring at the ceiling.

Rumors of the last production spread quickly and the next day crowds curious to see the Prince of Vleugel Academy in a bewitching goddess costume gathered outside the gates. And while the orphanage grounds were behind a fence, some overenthusiastic female fans had climbed over it to ask Cecilia for autographs, which only stressed her out more.

She glanced at the clock. There was about an hour left until the show. Getting her stage makeup done and costume put on would take some time, but she could afford to take a little break.

"Is it okay for me to come in, Cecil?" came a familiar voice along with a knock on the door.

Cecilia opened the door, surprised to see who was behind it.

"Grace? What are you doing here?"

"I had to talk to you. Lean told me I'd find you here."

Cecilia had never seen Grace outside her research lab before. On top of that, she was wearing a black dress instead of her lab coat this time, and she'd tied her unruly gray hair into a ponytail.

"I was told that you were on break. May I steal some of your time?"

"Sure, no problem! And I actually wanted to talk to you about something, too, so this is just perfect!"

Cecilia had been meaning to go and see Grace to get more info about Eins and Zwei. She was planning to hold off until after the shows, but since Grace was here, Cecilia thought she might as well ask her about them now.

Grace came into the room and sat down on the stool Cecilia offered her. Cecilia moved her chair to sit opposite her.

"Anyway, what did you want to talk about, Grace?"

"Well, I need to ask you about something."

"Yeah?"

"I asked Lean about it, too. Have you run into Prince Janis since Advent started, by any chance?"

"Wait, who's that? The final boss in Oscar's, Gil's, and Dante's storylines?"

"That's right."

Cecilia's jaw dropped. Prince Janis was the third son of the king of the neighboring country. He had amethyst eyes and hair as white as freshly fallen snow. He's an enemy in the game, one whose gentle looks and soft manner of speaking bely his inhuman cruelty. It is he who sends Dante to assassinate Oscar, but his motives are unknown. In fact, he's the most mysterious character in the game.

"I haven't met him. Why do you ask?"

"People are saying he's come to Prosper for Advent."

Cecilia searched her memory, but she couldn't remember any events featuring Prince Janis appearing at the festival.

Grace continued, her voice gravely serious.

"It was only after I heard that he might be here that I remembered that there is a bad ending branching off the protagonist's Advent encounter with Prince Janis."

She went on to explain that this was an extremely rare event that occurs only when the Holy Maiden candidate chosen for Advent celebrations doesn't have enough affection points for the normal route, and when one of the characters feels intense hatred for the protagonist.

In this bad ending, Prince Janis manipulates a bunch of different people to attack and kill Lean on Advent Day.

"The player knows Janis is behind it all in the game, but nobody else is aware of it..."

"So the blame gets pinned on me, and I get killed for it?"

Cecilia finished, and Grace nodded.

"But hold on, you said he uses a lot of people to pull that off? How is that possible? He may be a prince, but he's from a different country and has, like, zero influence over here, right?"

"Ah, I forgot to explain that!"

Grace clapped her hands.

"It's revealed in the True Love Route that Prince Janis has the power to cause Obstructions to possess people."

"Say whaaat?!" exclaimed Cecilia, aghast.

Grace calmly carried on.

"That ability doesn't work on everyone, though. Remember Oscar's route? At the end, you have to fight Prince Janis after an Obstruction possesses him, right? But when you're playing the same event while on the True Love Route, you find out that Janis summons the Obstruction himself to make him more powerful for that battle."

"Is that what happens?"

"You might have noticed that only people who talk with Prince Janis become possessed."

Now that Grace pointed it out, Cecilia realized it was true. She had no idea that Prince Janis was behind it when she was playing the game, so she hadn't made that connection at the time, but it should have rung alarm bells.

"At the end of the True Love Route, you fight Prince Janis, who lets the source of the Obstructions, which had been sealed deep in the shrine, possess him. If you manage to defeat him, he gets sealed, and the world is safe from Obstructions forever after. But if you lose, it's over not just for you but for the whole planet, too."

"You're making me seriously scared now, Grace."

"It's normal as far as games go. You lose to the final boss, and the world gets destroyed," she said matter-of-factly. "But I digress. The bad ending where Prince Janis and a possessed mob attack the

Holy Maiden candidate on parade is extremely rare. If there have been no harbingers yet, we need not worry."

She breathed deeply with relief. That seemed to be all she had to say. The disturbing possible future she described didn't seem to be in the cards after all.

"And what did you want to talk to me about, Cecilia?"

"Ah, right. So—"

Just then, however, they heard a woman's piercing scream. Cecilia and Grace looked at each other in alarm.

The scream came from the room where stage props and costumes were stored. Upon heading there, Cecilia and Grace learned that one of the troupe members went in to get something and made a horrifying discovery, which prompted the scream—someone had tampered with the goddess costume.

"That's unbelievable…"

"Who could have done it?"

The costume had been ripped to shreds and was splattered with red and yellow paint. In places, the two colors mixed to make orange.

In addition to Grace and Cecilia, Oscar and Gilbert also entered the room. They'd honored their promise and had come to help out that day. The pair had also heard the scream and came to see what happened.

"Lean's going to be heartbroken when she sees it…"

"I feel so sorry for her…"

Oscar and Gilbert gazed at the costume with pity in their eyes. They knew how much work Lean had put into making it.

The woman who found the goddess dress in this state had gone to fetch Lean, so it was just the four of them.

Cecilia stood before the dress with a grim look on her face.

"Do you think it's that bully's work again?"

"That seems likely, seeing as all of the other costumes are intact."

"Good point…"

If Cecil's fangirls managed to find their way into the orphanage grounds to pester Cecilia for autographs, a person with bad intentions could get inside, too.

Gilbert knelt on the floor to inspect the splotches of paint.

"It hasn't dried yet. The person who did this might still be nearby."

"How would we know who it is, though?"

Oscar knelt next to Gilbert and picked up the hem of the dress. Lean had stayed up late the previous night to sew in an additional layer of fabric under the thigh slits, but it was now in tatters. Oscar noticed something else, though.

"Hmm? Gilbert, look at this!"

"What have you got?"

"Footprints, I think."

He pointed to a spot on the floor near the hem of the dress. The culprit had stepped into a puddle of paint, leaving orange footprints.

"They almost blend in with the color of the floor. I guess they didn't realize they left a trail."

"If they were unaware of it, it might lead us to them."

"Assuming they haven't walked off very far, that is."

Oscar and Gilbert stood up at once and turned to Cecilia who'd just been standing there not sure what to do with herself.

"We're going to follow the footprints."

"I'll come with you!"

"Please stay here with Grace. Someone has to brief Lean when she gets here," Oscar stopped her in her tracks.

"All right," she agreed.

Cecilia was feeling a bit depressed about the whole thing and was worried that she'd only get in the way if she went along with the guys. She didn't have the mental strength at that moment to face the person who viciously ripped up her costume, if Oscar and Gilbert did find them.

The boys left, following the marks on the floor. Cecilia was now alone with Grace. She covered her face, looking distressed.

"It's my fault…"

"Don't blame yourself for what this person did. You haven't done anything wrong."

Cecilia thought Grace was just trying to cheer her up, because she was definitely the one to blame. This wouldn't have happened if she hadn't put off finding out who her bully was and dealing with them. She'd incorrectly assumed that it could wait until later, since the bullying was only affecting her.

Cecilia sensed someone's presence moments before they spoke.

"I heard about the dress and came here as quickly as I could…"

"Eins…"

"It's in a worse state than I imagined."

The actress who'd been the first to find the ruined costume must have told him about it. Eins saw how miserable Cecilia was looking and patted her on the back.

"Well, don't worry about it too much. By the way, do you have a minute?"

"I guess so?"

"I wanted to talk to you about Zwei."

He shot Grace a glance, signaling that he wanted to have his conversation with Cecil without anyone else present. She understood immediately.

"Don't worry about me."

"We could go over to the next room to talk, if you want?" suggested Cecilia.

"Yeah, that works."

Eins was acting atypically serious. Cecilia turned back to Grace before leaving with him.

"Sorry, Grace. I'll be back in a bit."

"Okay."

Cecilia and Eins walked out of the room together.

It didn't take long at all for Oscar and Gilbert to track down their quarry.

"I heard about you from Gilbert. So now you're in the business of destroying costumes, too?"

They were in the temporary storage room. The culprits were shivering on the floor, looking up at Oscar and Gilbert with fear. The soles of their shoes were caked with paint.

There was the burly upstarts' kid. The all brawn, no brain thug. And lastly, the sidekick who saw bullying others as the sole purpose of his existence. The gang of three bullies who used to target Zwei.

"Have you been holding a grudge against Cecil ever since he stood up against you?"

"Do you have any idea the mistake you've made by harassing him?"

Against the furious glare of Oscar, who was enraged that they had been tormenting his darling fiancée, and Gilbert's terrifyingly frigid stare, the three bullies huddled together and whimpered pathetically.

"I knew you weren't the brightest crayons in the box, but you've shown us today that your stupidity is truly exceptional."

"Not only have you been playing mean pranks on Cecil at school, but you threw an egg at him at the parade, tried to drop a flowerpot on his head, hit him with a bucket of hot water, and now you've destroyed his stage costume?"

"Th-that wasn't us!" shouted the upstarts' kid, whose name was Derek. His lackeys, Kevin and Skeet, also piped up.

"Y-yeah! We only did stuff like putting dead bugs and dirty rags in Cecil's school bag. And we did throw that egg at him. too!"

"We didn't throw no flowerpots on anyone! And we didn't rip the dress neither! We were gonna mess with it, but it was already torn up when we got there!"

Oscar and Gilbert exchanged glances. It would've been obvious they were lying if they denied all of it, but why were they owning up to some of the incidents?

"There's no way we'd drop a flowerpot on someone! Or hit someone with a bucket of hot water! That sort of stuff is, like, serious!"

"And threatening to stab Cecil wasn't serious?"

"That was just to scare him! You can't stab anyone with my knife, anyway. Look!"

Kevin took a dagger out of his pocket and pressed the blade with one finger. It retracted into the hilt. It was just like the theater props.

"My dad's been making gadgets like these since he retired. These gimmick daggers can't hurt anyone!"

He threw the blade over to Oscar and Gilbert so they could see for themselves if they wanted to.

"So, like, okay, some threats, some kicking and punching maybe, we did that. But we wouldn't do anything that would seriously hurt someone!"

"Or kill them!"

"Yeah! Whoever's been throwing pots at people is just insane!"

"Right. You're bully boys, not thugs who'd do anything dangerous."

Oscar's remark struck a nerve, and Derek did his best to appear intimidating as he growled back.

"Say what?! We ARE dangerous, dammit!"

He couldn't fool anyone, though. He and his gang were clearly just adolescent boys who'd naively tried to act tougher than they were.

Gilbert toyed with the knife, pushing the blade in and letting it slide back out, thinking.

"If they're not lying, then who dropped that flowerpot? And tore the dress?"

"Gilbert! Oscar! Where are you?!"

They heard Grace's panicked voice, almost a scream, from the corridor, so they stuck their heads out of the room. Grace saw them and hurried over, with Lean and Eins in tow.

"What's the matter?"

"Wait, where's Cecil?" asked Oscar.

Eins, pale as a sheet and with eyes darting this way and that, answered him.

"Zwei, he… He impersonated me and…and he…abducted Cecil…"

Cecilia slowly opened her eyes a crack and saw wooden beams above her. It was semi-dark in the room. Rain pattered against a small window near her head. She shuddered, breathing in the heavy, humid air, finally regaining her consciousness fully.

Right, now I remember what happened…

Still lying down, she twisted her body to look around. Her wrists were bound with rope, and her stomach ached from being punched.

She was in a small log house, or rather, a hunting lodge. There were traps, snares, and coils of rope lying around.

Not this again…

It was just like when Heimat abducted her. It felt like that happened a long time ago, but it wasn't even half a year.

She leaned against the wall to help herself sit up. At least her legs weren't tied.

"You're awake."

She looked in the direction of the voice, and a petite shape emerged from the shadows. The rain had stopped, and a streak of moonlight shone through the window, falling on the bottom half of the boy's face in a rather creepy fashion. Cecilia spoke to him.

"I don't understand why you're doing this, Zwei."

He sucked in his breath when she spoke his name.

"You knew it was me? And there I was, feeling absolutely confident my Eins impression was spot on."

"I thought you were him right until you attacked me. I did suspect that you had ripped up the dress, though. It seemed like something you might do."

He looked unsettled when she said that, which confirmed her suspicions. She had just been testing the waters with that accusation after having a very vague hunch about him.

"What made you think that?" he asked quietly.

After a moment of silence, Cecilia spoke, choosing her words carefully.

"The dress was ripped, not cut. There were all sorts of stage props lying around, and Lean left her sewing kit there, too. It would be easy to pick up scissors or a knife to quickly destroy it, but for whatever reason, the perpetrator chose to use their own hands. Then it hit me—perhaps they couldn't use sharp objects."

"You're more observant than I gave you credit for, Cecil."

Zwei smiled. The upper half of his face was concealed in the darkness, so Cecilia couldn't make out his expression, but he had curled his lips into a gentle arch.

Cecilia bit her lower lip, her worst fears about him proven right on point.

"So it was you bullying me all along?"

"Yes, it was me for the most part."

"And why did you do that?"

"I didn't like you getting close."

"Close to what?"

"To us."

He covered his face with both hands, as if he were in pain. Perhaps it was an expression of regret.

"Do you remember the conversation about people believing that twins are cursed, Cecil?"

She remembered it very clearly. It took place the day after she failed at cooking that custard and was in a very low mood. Coco and Zwei happened to find her sitting on a bench.

"It wasn't me you talked to that day. It was Eins."

"What?"

"He wanted to see for himself what you were like, so I let him take my place. Only, I wasn't expecting him to tell you that some people think we're devil spawn."

Cecilia guessed from his manner that Eins had shared the memories of that day with him, so that she wouldn't accidentally find out they'd switched places...

"Did you notice then how Eins enjoyed talking to you? I asked him about it, I wanted him to tell me what he thought. And he smiled and said that you weren't a bad person after all. In fact, he said you were fun!"

Zwei's voice grew louder, even aggressive, as he became more emotional. He was no longer the soft-spoken, calm boy she had known.

"It was the first time Eins had showed interest in someone besides me! I was so confused, I didn't know what to do with myself!"

"So you tried to drop a flowerpot on my head?"

Thinking back, the bullying had started the night after she had that chat with Eins impersonating Zwei.

"That was an accident. I was watching you from a window, and I accidentally knocked down the flowerpot with my elbow. But it made me think that maybe you'd stop meddling with us if this sort of thing kept happening."

And that's why Zwei had kept harassing her. How she was supposed to understand that it was all a message telling her to keep away from the twins was a mystery, though.

He carried on.

"But whatever I did, you just ignored it and kept getting in the way! Eins started to change, and all he talked about was you!"

"Um, Zwei…"

"The two of us were one! Until you ruined everything by butting in where you weren't wanted!"

Zwei lost control of his emotions, shouting at her while holding his head. It really looked bizarre, as if he was being tormented by something possessing him.

"Calm down, Zwei! You're acting crazy today! What's gotten into you?!"

"I'm not crazy!"

He pushed her down onto the floor and sat on her torso. Then he tightened his hands around her neck.

"Do I look insane to you, huh? You made me this way!"

He squeezed her neck. Unable to breathe, Cecilia flailed her legs in panic.

"Let…go…"

"I only have Eins! He was all I had, until you turned up to steal him from me!"

Suffocating, Cecilia shut her eyes. Suddenly, she felt a warm droplet hit her eyelid. She forced her eyes to open a little and saw that Zwei's emerald eyes were brimming with tears. And on his right eye was a strange mark…

I know what that is!

177

Symbols like that appeared only on the bodies of people possessed by Obstructions.

"Where the hell could they be?!"

Oscar was losing his nerve. More than ten hours had passed since Cecilia and Zwei vanished without a trace. Oscar, Gilbert, Eins, and Grace had been searching for them the entire time. The night was drawing to an end, and the light of dawn was peeking over the horizon.

"We haven't searched the south side yet. Let's go there next," Gilbert motioned with his finger, his voice hoarse and face drenched in sweat.

Grace, who also had beads of sweat on her face, sounded exhausted as she asked:

"Eins, is there any other place you can think of where Zwei could have taken Cecil?"

"No! Do you think I wouldn't have told you at the start if there was?!"

Lean had been helping them with the search, too, until about an hour earlier. As the Holy Maiden candidate, she had to go offer her prayers on the dawn of Advent Day. Doctor Mordred came to fetch her, and she'd left with him. She hadn't really wanted to be dragged off to the ritual since she was so worried about her friend, but Doctor Mordred warned her that Cecil would be held responsible for her neglecting this important duty once he was found.

Gilbert had linked up with Grace while the search party was running around.

"Do you really have no idea where they are?" he asked so quietly only she could hear him.

"The location for Zwei's bad ending is picked at random. I

checked the ones I knew about already. Also, we can't be sure that this is actually the bad ending."

The current situation had significantly diverged from the scenario she was familiar with. There was no performance at the orphanage in the game to begin with, so obviously there was no event in which Zwei kidnaps the protagonist after leaving the props room. The story branch leading to the bad ending took place later in the game.

In other words, what was happening now was a completely original twist of fate after Grace and Cecilia altered the expected flow of events.

Another hour passed, and the main streets of the city had slowly started filling up with people, but Cecilia and Zwei were nowhere to be found. Oscar, Grace, Gilbert, and Eins had checked everywhere they could think of, but the two had disappeared without a trace.

They could scarcely feel their legs after an entire night frantically running around. Even Oscar, who was the most physically fit of them, was worn out. Eins bowed his head in abject apology.

"It's my fault! I noticed Zwei had been acting strange, but I ignored it..."

He told them that Zwei's behavior had abruptly changed three days earlier. Eins had been on a walk with Cecil, and as soon as he came back home, Zwei pounced on him with questions about where he'd been and who he'd been with. It was no secret, so Eins told Zwei that he'd been with Cecil—and that sent his brother into a fury. Frenzied, he begged Eins to never see Cecil again.

"At the time I thought that maybe he wasn't feeling well, but he actually looked like something was tormenting him or like he'd gone crazy."

Eins bit his lower lip, the regret over not having taken action earlier unbearable for him. Oscar patted him on the back.

"This isn't the time to obsess over what you could've done differently. We have to concentrate on finding your brother and Cecil."

"The city's gotten busy. Two of us should continue searching, while the other two ask around if anyone's seen Cecil or Zwei." The action-oriented Gilbert helped break the impasse as the others were feeling overwhelmed by powerlessness.

"Good idea. I suppose I could mobilize the soldiers under my command, too."

"...Please do," Gilbert nodded with a heavy heart.

Oscar's proposal would expose Cecil's true identity. A baron's son not coming home for a night was no reason to mobilize the army. But the prince's fiancée going missing was a different story.

"Hello," came a voice from behind Eins.

They turned to find a young man smiling pleasantly at them. He had the hood of his cloak up, but strands of his brown hair were poking out from under it. The man's eyes were like amethysts. Another man was standing behind him, presumably his companion. He was of a similar age, with long black hair.

He's got purple eyes?

Gilbert furrowed his brow at the sight of the man. Purple was an unusual eye color in these parts. Pale purple was fairly common in the neighboring country of Nortracha, but even there, only the royal family boasted deep amethyst eyes like this man's.

No way...

Gilbert didn't like where this was going. He'd heard that the third prince of a certain country had vagabond tendencies and would secretly wander from one land to another. He was supposed to have hair as white as freshly fallen snow, but hair color could be easily changed.

If that was him...

"It's good to see you again."

The purple-eyed man smiled at Eins. Gilbert noted with surprise that they knew each other somehow.

"You seem to be looking for something?"

Eins was a bit thrown for a moment, before replying in all eagerness:

"Right, you know him! Have you seen Cec—?"

"Eins, no."

Oscar interrupted him, pulling him back by his arm. He stepped forward to face the mysterious man.

"And what might you be doing here, Prince Janis?"

Eins startled upon hearing the name, while Gilbert's expression just grew darker as his suspicions were confirmed. Though he'd never been outside the country, he was well aware of Janis' bad reputation.

The prince had reportedly broken the neck of a minister who stole funds from the national coffers. He'd cut off the arm of a princess who'd been sent to him as a potential bride, just for fun. Once, he told a man who'd lost his child that he knew the killer, pointing out a completely innocent person to him, and watched as the grief-stricken father murdered them. Prince Janis' name always came up in the context of horrific tales like that.

"Well, well, I see that my disguise can't fool you, Prince Oscar! I'm here to see the sights. Your Advent festival is famous, after all."

"And why are you without escort?"

"Unlike you, I'm only the third in line to the throne, so nobody sees me as a person of importance. I don't require an entourage of guards to ensure my safety." He smiled as if it didn't bother him in the slightest.

This is the worst possible time for him to turn up...

The unexpected appearance of the foreign prince vexed Gilbert. This was the last thing he needed when he and his friends had a matter of utmost urgency to attend to. Even assuming the events unfolding now weren't consistent with Zwei's bad ending in the game, he feared that something horrible would happen if they didn't find Cecilia soon.

That said, Janis was a visiting prince from a neighboring country. Putting the matter of whether he'd arrived by legal means or not aside, it would be quite an affront to tell him to enjoy the festival and leave him like that. They would be obligated to show him the sights should he request them to do so.

I can't afford to stick around…

Gilbert frantically thought of an excuse to get away. Oscar could certainly handle the other prince on his own, and it would not be disrespectful to leave the two royals to keep each other company. He'd only need a convincing excuse to leave now.

His chain of thought was interrupted when he noticed that Grace was standing there, looking absolutely appalled.

"It's really happening…"

"Grace, what's wrong?"

Grace, shaking, grabbed him by the lapels.

"Gilbert, if I'm not mistaken about this, Lean may be in grave danger!"

No sooner had she said that than Prince Janis spoke up.

"Oh, and by the way," he said with undisguised joy, "there's been quite the commotion over there just a while earlier. You know, where the Holy Maiden was doing that special ritual of some sort? There might still be some amusement to be had…if you hurry."

With a flash of panic in her eyes, Grace broke into a run.

Just as Cecilia was about to lose consciousness from lack of oxygen, Zwei relaxed his grip on her neck. She opened her eyes a little and looked at his emerald pupils, dilating and contracting as the emotions of rage, regret, and guilt vied for domination. Before she could say anything to him, though, he choked her again.

This cycle repeated for hours, over and over again. Both victim and attacker were at their limit. Cecilia kept drifting in and out of awareness, the mark on Zwei's eye there for her to see whenever she managed to lift her eyelids.

I didn't know Obstructions could manifest in this way...

Surprisingly, she felt no resentment toward Zwei as he sat there on top of her and choked her out. She felt neither anger nor resentment because she believed that he didn't really want to kill her. He couldn't bring himself to carry out the deed even under the possession of the Obstruction.

If I could just touch that mark, I'd be able to free him...

Alas, her hands were tied. She had nothing to cut the rope with, and she didn't have any other way of loosening it, either. She was entirely powerless, barely coming to whenever Zwei thought to let her breathe for a moment.

"Can I ask you something?" Cecilia managed to croak out when another brief moment of respite came. With Zwei's strength faltering, she thought he might be in a state of mind to listen. And she was right—he looked at her in surprise and after a brief pause asked, "What is it?"

"Why did you pose as Eins when you came to see me?"

"Why? Because you wouldn't have come with me if you knew it was me."

"Why did you think that?"

"Because I know you hate me."

His assertion baffled Cecilia. She couldn't remember saying or doing anything that might make Zwei think that. In fact, she thought they were getting along just fine.

"I know you and Eins have been saying nasty things about me behind my back."

"That's not true!"

"Liar!"

He choked her again, but his grip was weak, so she could still breathe. Maybe he hadn't recovered from his last exhausting bout of rage yet.

"I know it's true, because someone overheard you and told me about it!"

Three days earlier, a stranger had approached Zwei. The man had brown hair and was wearing a hood pulled down low over his face. He narrowed his purple eyes when he saw Zwei, then greeted the boy as if he knew him.

It transpired that the man had become acquainted with Eins and Cecil after running into them earlier. He'd mistaken Zwei for Eins just now.

"Eins is my older brother. We're twins."

"Ah, so *you're* his brother…"

He placed emphasis on "you," as if he'd heard about Zwei. The latter guessed that Cecil and Eins had mentioned him to the man, so he asked about it, not suspecting anything. But the man winced uncomfortably.

"No, they hadn't told me about you, but your name came up in their conversation that, as chance would have it, I happened to be within earshot of. It was rather disturbing, so it left an impression on me."

"Disturbing? And you're sure they were talking about me?"

"Well, maybe I misheard. You do seem like a rather nice person, after all."

Zwei couldn't leave it at that.

"No, tell me, what did they say about me?"

"Please don't hold it against me," the man began cautiously. "But I heard them saying you…"

* * *

"...Left...your mother...to die," Zwei repeated haltingly.

"We didn't say that!" Cecilia screamed.

"Really? Then how did he know about my mother?! Only you and Eins know what happened to her!" Zwei yelled back, his voice distorted by his sobbing.

Cecilia remembered that she did talk about his mother with Eins three days earlier, shortly after they met that man who supposedly overheard them.

"I think I've seen that guy before."

"Really?"

"In Cuddy's house... I don't know, maybe he just looked similar."

Was that...him?

The man's appearance was unforgettable. Amethyst eyes and brown hair, with a face so handsome he should have been one of the love interests in the game. Why did she have a nagging feeling that she'd seen him somewhere before?

Maybe she saw someone just like him in the game, but with white hair, not brown. Dressed in a more royal outfit...

Th-that's Prince Janis!

She finally connected all the dots. And according to Grace, Prince Janis had the ability to make Obstructions possess people...

Is that why Zwei got possessed?

It seemed highly likely that Prince Janis had induced Zwei's possession. Could the prince also have been responsible for summoning the Obstruction that had caused Cuddy to murder Eins and Zwei's mother?

"I don't want to hurt you, Cecil. I actually, I..."

"Zwei, calm down and listen—"

"But that man said… He said you were going to turn Eins against me!"

Dark miasma gushed out of Zwei's body, and he clasped his hands tighter than ever before around Cecilia's neck.

"Everyone thinks…that I'm in the way! Dad, all our servants, they all think I should have gotten killed instead of mom! If only I was dead. Then nobody would call Eins devil spawn anymore, and you and him would both be better off without me, too!"

The pressure around Cecilia's neck disappeared again. She opened her eyes and saw Zwei covering his face with his hands.

"Right…"

It sounded like Zwei had realized something. He stood up, got off Cecilia, and walked on unsteady feet over to a table, resting a hand on it for support.

"It's clear to me what I have to do now."

"Zwei, what are you—?"

"It's not you who has to die. It's me."

He was still holding a hand over his face, but Cecilia could see between his fingers that the mark of the Obstruction was spreading like a poisonous vine. It covered most of the right side of his visage.

Zwei moved his free hand over the table, as if groping for something. Suddenly, his hand stopped, and she figured that he'd found the thing he was looking for.

"I have to die. That way I won't have to hurt you, and I won't cause any more trouble for Eins, either. He'll be be so much happier once I'm gone."

"Zwei, no!"

He was holding a knife, the kind hunters used to skin their prey. Though his hand was trembling, he didn't seem frightened by the blade. His suicidal drive, amplified by the Obstruction, was stronger than even the trauma he'd suffered witnessing his mother's murder.

Zwei pointed the blade at his neck. His breathing was erratic, but unlike when he'd been choking Cecilia, he wasn't hesitating in the slightest.

"I'm sorry for hurting you, Cecil."

He braced himself for the pain that was sure to come when he slit his throat...

"I'm not letting you do this!"

Cecilia headbutted Zwei, sending him to the ground. Then she kicked the knife out of his hand. It skidded on the floor and came to rest under a cupboard.

"What are you doing, Cecil?!"

"Shut up!"

This time it was Cecilia who sat down on top of Zwei. Then she bent as far backward as she could without losing balance and... slammed her head into his, hard.

They both blacked out, their foreheads bruised red at the point of impact. Cecilia recovered first. She checked to make sure that the mark on Zwei's face was completely gone.

Looks like I did it.

She sighed deeply in relief, got off Zwei, and slumped to the floor. That might have been a rather crude way to deal with the Obstruction, but it did the trick.

"I'm so done with today! No more!"

All the muscles in her body went slack as sweat gushed out of her every pore. She took another deep breath and slowly exhaled all the air in her lungs. Zwei, who was lying on the floor beside her, finally came round and spoke to her in a tired voice.

"What were you thinking...?"

"You okay now, Zwei?"

"Mentally, yeah."

"And physically?"

"I feel awful."

He stood up and walked over to her to untie her hands.

She'd been bound for so long that the ropes had left red marks over her wrists and even a few blisters. Zwei winced when he noticed that.

"I don't understand what came over me. Why was I so angry? Why was I trying to kill you? Eins must be so worried about us. And the others, too…"

He sat down by a wall, pulling his knees up to make himself look small.

"I actually want to kill myself even more now," he whispered.

Cecilia slapped him on the head.

"Don't you say that."

"But Cecil…"

"Lots of people die despite not wanting to. Lots of people don't survive despite desperately wanting to live!"

Zwei looked up at Cecilia. She smiled at him, wishing to give him courage.

"Your mother sacrificed her life to save yours, and Eins has been protecting you ever since then. So don't throw your life away! Think of how much it would hurt the people who care about you!"

She sat down next to Zwei on the floor, then leaned against him so that their heads touched.

"And if you ever feel like it's getting to be too much for you, you can talk to me about it. I'll listen. Just don't talk like your life means nothing!"

"Okay."

"You promise?"

"Yes," he nodded.

"Good!"

Cecilia smiled widely at him, and although Zwei had his knees pulled up to his chin, she glimpsed a little smile on his face, too.

"Whoa, it's morning already!"

"Do you think Eins and your friends have been looking for us?"

"It's a fair bet!"

The sun was already quite high above the horizon. It was dawn when she first came to, but she hadn't really noticed how much time passed throughout the whole ordeal.

Something tells me people will be mad at me...

Cecilia gave a self-deprecating smile. It had been many hours since Zwei led her away. Someone must have noticed that they were gone. Their friends might have been searching for them, worried about their safety.

Also, it was Advent Day. Cecilia should have greeted the sunrise together with Lean, who was offering prayers at the official ceremony. That was her duty as one of the knights.

There's seven of us, so I'm sure it went okay even with me missing... Oh, hold on...

Suddenly, she had a nagging feeling that she was forgetting something important. She stared at the ceiling and searched her memory... Then her face froze, all of the blood draining out of it. She stood up abruptly.

"Crap!"

"What's wrong?"

"I forgot about Lean! She's in danger!"

Cecilia's lower lip quivered. The conversation she'd had with Grace played back in her mind.

"I remembered that there is a bad ending branching off the protagonist's Advent encounter with Prince Janis."

That route would be triggered if the Holy Maiden candidate performing Advent rituals didn't have enough affection points with any of the knights to unlock the normal route and was also the object of one of the character's ire. Now that Cecilia thought about it, those conditions could apply to Lean. And the branching point...

I have met Prince Janis!

Occasionally, Cecilia would inadvertently do something required of the protagonist to trigger progression through the story, and the narrative would still move forward. It was possible that her encounter with Prince Janice could do the same.

"Where are we, Zwei? How far are we from Algram?"

"Um, about two hours' journey on foot."

"Two hours?! We won't make it in time!"

There was no time to spare if the bad ending was already unfolding. It might already be too late. It *definitely* would be in two hours. Cecilia panicked.

"Do you want to go to where Lean is?" Zwei asked her quietly.

She nodded, and he stood up.

"All right. I'll send you there right away."

Cecilia widened her eyes at him. She didn't have the slightest clue as to how that would be possible. Zwei touched his Artifact.

"Our true ability actually isn't Sharing."

Advent Day morning prayers took place in a plaza at the very center of Algram. A special wooden platform about twice the height of a man had been set up there for the prayer leader.

Tradition had it that the Holy Maiden would start the day with a morning prayer every thirty-first of October, acting as a proxy for the goddess. The worshippers, all dressed in white, would listen in reverent silence. As soon as the long prayer came to an end, however, joyous and raucous festivities would begin.

* * *

But on this Advent Day, the central plaza was noisy for an entirely different reason.

"Abolish the Church of Caritade!"

"The Holy Maiden serves the Devil!"

Amid screams of shock and indignation, people opposed to the Church of Caritade had organized themselves into a mob and were clambering onto the speaker's platform. They wore red kerchiefs around their necks and wooden masks over their faces, and were armed with farm tools, such as spades and hoes. But what stood out the most about the rioters was that they were all emanating a dark and sinister miasma. Each and every one of them was possessed by an Obstruction.

"What's happening here?" Oscar groaned as he took in the scene before him.

The poorly trained soldiers employed by the Church were just barely managing to keep the rioters wielding farm tools at bay. Unfortunately, the hired hands were both outnumbered and clearly struggling. Some of Lean's classmates stood on the platform facing outward, trying to keep the violent agitators at bay. Some of the worshippers stayed behind to watch the fighting, while others were frantically trying to push their way through the crowd to get away from danger.

Oscar was lost for words as he tried to make sense of what was going on.

"Oscar! Gil!"

Jade waved to them. The two boys rushed over to where he was standing together with Mordred. Both the doctor and Jade also looked like they were on their last legs.

"You're finally here!"

"What the hell is going on, Jade?" Gilbert asked, stone-faced.

Holding back tears, Jade filled them in on the events from that morning.

"Lean was offering her prayers when that anti-Caritade mob suddenly pushed through to the platform and started attacking the believers! They're all under the influence of Obstructions! The gendarmerie arrived shortly, but there's too few of them…"

"They were totally disorganized engaging the rioters. It's only thanks to Dante and Huey that they're still holding out."

Mordred and Jade were completely shattered, so they must have done their fair share of fighting, too.

Just then, a body skidded across the ground and came to a halt right in front of them. It was one of the rioters, still alive. Though a red handkerchief was still fixed about their neck, their mask had been torn off to reveal the mark of an Obstruction on their cheek. And the person who kneeled on his chest and bent down to touch the mark was…

"Dante!"

"Oscar! Better late than never! Boy, am I glad to see you here!" Dante grinned, his cheeks speckled with blood.

"Where have you been?"

Huey emerged from the brawl next. He was holding onto one of the possessed rioters, who was snarling like a wild animal. The man's arms and legs must have been dislocated, for he was unable to move. As with the other rioter, he bore the mark of an Obstruction on his face. Perhaps the rioters were wearing masks to conceal them.

Huey pushed the man toward Jade.

"Jade, you got this."

"S-sure!"

Jade touched the mark on the man's face, and he immediately stopped growling, falling unconscious. Mordred set to tending to the man's injuries at once. Huey wasn't a knight, so he had to send the rioters he'd rendered harmless to Jade to free them from the Obstructions.

Oscar couldn't help but feel guilty as he realized how much effort his friends had put into keeping the situation under control in his absence. He approached Dante, who'd been cracking his neck, ready to leap into the fray.

"I'm sorry I wasn't here to help."

"Aw, don't worry about me. You've been busy with something else, right? I take it Cecil's disappeared again?"

Dante looked around past Oscar as if he was expecting to see Cecil there. Oscar's expression clouded over.

"We haven't found him yet," he murmured.

Dante fell silent for a moment, but then he smiled softly and patted Oscar on the shoulder.

"Ah. Well, why don't we finish up here first and then look for Cecil together? Is that all right with you, too, Gil?"

Dante still had his hand placed reassuringly on Oscar's shoulder, but he was looking past him, at Gilbert. Oscar turned to see Gilbert nod gravely in assent.

"That's fine by me. We've already tried and failed to locate Cecil by ourselves, so we either need more people to help, or we'll have to change our approach. Obviously, we can't recruit anyone else to lend a hand before we resolve the situation here, so that should be our priority."

"Huh, I was expecting you to throw a tantrum but, look at you, so calm and collected."

"Dante!" Oscar scolded his friend for taunting Gilbert, whose patience was running out even before Dante's jeer.

"Really? You think this is me being calm and collected?"

"Aw, don't get prickly, Gil. I was complimenting your ability to keep up appearances."

Dante turned away from them and began stretching, as if he was warming up for a workout.

"So what's the plan? Even with you here, we're badly out-numbered. If this fighting drags on too long, we'll lose for sure. Huey and I can't use all the skills in our arsenal with so many eyes on us, nor can we lead Lean to safety when there's an angry mob blocking the plaza."

"We'll need to increase our numbers, then," replied Gilbert.

"How?" Dante asked, looking at him questioningly.

"By setting fire to the hay bales at the plaza stables. Even people who are too far to hear the commotion here will see the smoke. Most buildings around this area are built from wood, so the gen-darmerie is sure to rush over."

"But will they be capable of putting a stop to this if they're only expecting a fire?"

"His Highness can see to it that they are useful."

They all looked at Oscar.

"You want ME to command them?"

"While I can't vouch for the nobles, the gendarmerie will certainly accept your authority. They wouldn't dare challenge the crown prince, even if a commanding officer shows up eventually."

"Assuming they accept me, what am I supposed to order them to do? They can't exorcise Obstructions."

Dante stroked his chin in thought.

"They could tie up the rioters for us to exorcise later."

"I imagine it'd take at least three officers to subdue a single rioter, and who's to say that another one won't attack them while they're occupied? That means we would need four gendarmes per rioter."

"We won't be able to secure that many, will we..." Gilbert conceded.

Oscar felt a tug at his sleeve. It was Jade trying to get his atten-tion. He and Eins had approached the prince, looking very earnest.

"Might this help?" Jade pointed to a large net made from rope.

"We could cast that net over them to trap a bunch of rioters at once, then tie them up individually? That won't require nearly as many people to pull off, right?"

"Where did you get that from?" asked Oscar, walking over to them to examine the net. Jade glanced at a nearby general store.

"From that shop over there. I noticed they were selling deer leather products, so I went over to check their workshop at the back and found this by the hunting gear. Eins helped me carry it."

Eins and Jade must have gotten there just in time to overhear the others talking about their battle plan.

Dante patted Jade on the back with so much force, he nearly knocked him over.

"Excellent thinking! This is exactly what we need!"

Jade groaned but pushed his chest out proudly nonetheless... before he winced and shouted, "Please stop hurting me!"

Oscar unfolded the net on the ground. It was very wide, designed for catching large animals. It could probably hold ten rioters. Still...

"We don't have enough people."

"How many more do you suppose we need?" asked Gilbert.

"I'd say at least ten, maybe fifteen. Twenty to really tip the odds in our favor," Oscar replied grimly.

The net was a lucky find, but just one wasn't enough to make up for the fact that they were severely outnumbered. Just as they started to lose spirit, Eins quietly offered a suggestion.

"What if we had more nets?"

"Do you know where to find more?"

Oscar, still kneeling by the net, gazed up at him with faint hope in his eyes.

"No," Eins shook his head. Then he pointed at his bracelet. "But I can make them."

*　*　*

From there, everything went according to plan. The smoke attracted a bunch of gendarmes. Oscar took command of them. Gilbert signaled to the rooftop team to drop the big nets, while Dante and Huey engaged the mob on the ground level in battle. Mordred and Grace provided medical care, while Jade made sure the civilians evacuated the area. Eins stayed at Oscar's side, duplicating nets.

The racket died down half an hour later as they captured the last of the rioters. Several people were wounded, but there were no fatalities. They achieved total victory. All they had to do now was exorcise the Obstructions, one by one.

Some of the people who'd fled earlier came back to see the aftermath.

"Who would have guessed that Eins' special ability was Duplication," Jade said as he sat down next to Oscar. The prince had mud on his cheek; he must have fallen down at some point.

Oscar smiled awkwardly at Jade, who looked as if he might pass out on the ground at any moment. Then he directed his gaze at Eins, who was still panting from exerting himself during the operation.

"Didn't you say that your special ability was Sharing?"

"It is *our* special ability, my brother's and mine. It's something that we use together. But my actual ability is Duplication."

"Wait, so does Zwei also have his own skill?" asked Jade.

"Yeah," Eins gave a monosyllabic answer.

The mention of Zwei made Oscar instantly think of Cecilia. Where had she been since Zwei spirited her away somewhere the previous evening? Was she okay? Based on what Eins had said, Zwei had been mentally unstable for the last few days. He felt threatened by Cecilia and feared she was going to steal his dear brother from him. It was all too easy to guess why he'd abducted her.

I've got to stop thinking about it...

He shook his head as to banish the worst-possible scenarios from playing out in his head. Despite his wishes, however, his mind kept conjuring gruesome images of Cecilia getting hurt.

It was Dante's voice that brought him back to reality.

"Okay, it's time we move on to finding Zwei and Cecil!" Dante was raring to go as usual. He patted Oscar on the back and added, pointing at his hand, "Make sure you show that to the doc later."

Oscar looked at his hand, not understanding what Dante was talking about. Only then did he realize that he'd been clenching his fist so tight that his fingernails had dug deep into the palm of his hand, breaking the skin and making it bleed.

I'm being pathetic...

It had been drilled into him over and over again that he needed to maintain his composure no matter the circumstances. But it seemed impossible to keep a cool head when his fiancée was in danger.

"Hey, so, can I get Lean down now or what?"

Oscar looked up from his hand and over at Huey, who came after Dante.

"Yes, get her down."

They had left her up on the platform until now because they'd needed her to act as a decoy, grabbing the attention of the possessed rioters as Oscar and his team worked on capturing them.

We'll get Lean down and have her join our search for Cecilia.

But he'd let his guard down too soon.

"Abolish the Church of Caritade!"

A man was running toward the platform with a knife in one hand—possibly one of the daggers they'd used to cut rope—and a bottle with a burning rag stuck into it in the other. It was an

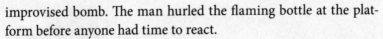

improvised bomb. The man hurled the flaming bottle at the platform before anyone had time to react.

"Aaargh!"

Lean screamed as the steps leading onto the platform caught fire. Mere moments later, it was engulfed in flames.

"Lean!"

"No, don't go there!"

"Let go of me!"

Oscar could see Dante and Huey arguing out of the corner of his eye. Jade was freaking out.

"Wh-what do we do now? Lean… Lean is up there…"

Oscar looked around desperately but couldn't find anything that he could use to put out the flames.

What now…?

The flames encircling Lean were creeping up toward her. Just then, Oscar noticed Eins moving his lips. He was muttering something.

"…was here."

"What was that, Eins?"

"If only Zwei was here. Then we could save her."

He curled his hands into fists and slammed them into the ground.

"Where the hell is he?!"

Just as he shouted that, the platform Lean was on was bathed in bright light.

It was like a scene straight out of the very last part of the national legend—familiar to even children in the Kingdom of Prosper—where the goddess is trapped between infernal flames. But then, a young man who would later become the first king of the nation saves her.

A prince did appear, with honey-blond hair and sapphire

eyes. Cecil jumped off the burning platform carrying Lean in her white Holy Maiden robe. He landed lightly on his feet and helped the shaking girl stand. There was a smidge of soot on her cheek, which he wiped with his thumb. Then he smiled a shatteringly beautiful smile of pure relief.

"Thankfully, I made it just in time."

Applause swept through the plaza.

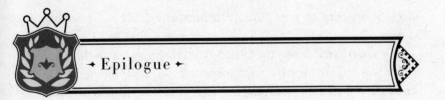

"So what you're saying is that you had such a great time together that you left the production site and went off to hang around somewhere else for the entire night, but then you realized that Lean was in danger, so Zwei used his teleportation ability to get you to her?"

"Yup!"

It had taken all evening to exorcise the rebels. Cecilia and Zwei were sitting on their knees on the floor in the academy lounge. Gilbert was sitting in a chair in front of them, looking very fed up. Behind him were Oscar and Dante, and even farther back was Eins, who was hanging his head despondently.

Nobody was forcing Cecilia and Zwei to prostrate themselves before Gilbert as he interrogated them—they'd chosen to sit that way.

"And you seriously want me to believe that?"

"Y-yes!" Cecilia replied in a louder voice, sitting up straighter.

Gilbert frowned and rubbed his forehead. He sighed loudly as he glanced again at the glaringly obvious red mark around Cecilia's neck.

"And how will you explain—?"

"It-it's all my fault! I'm so sorry!" Zwei cut Gilbert off. He bowed his head low in apology. "I got this idea in my head that

Cecil was going to take Eins from me, and I... I did horrible things..."

"It wasn't you! It was the Obstruction making you do that!"

"I was bullying you before it possessed me!" Zwei shouted back, and then he bit his lip. He hung his head even lower, on the verge of tears. "I'm so sorry about everything. What I did was unacceptable. Turn me in to the gendarmerie...it's what I deserve."

"I also apologize. I'm to blame, too," said Eins, sitting down next to his brother. He put his hand on the back of Zwei's head and pushed it down until his forehead touched the floor, then bowed just as deeply himself.

"If Zwei is to be punished, then you'll have to punish me, too. I'm responsible for not having stopped him," Eins said solemnly.

"But Eins...," his brother objected in a softer voice, but Eins just smiled at him with sorrow in his eyes.

"Your sins are my sins. We are one."

"I'm so sorry, Eins..."

Zwei began sobbing, and big teardrops rolled down his cheeks. He started wiping them with his sleeves, only for Eins to stop him and scold him gently.

"Don't, you'll make your face red."

The sight was so moving to Cecilia that tears welled up in her eyes. But not everyone found it heartwarming.

"Saying you're sorry isn't enough to get abduction, unlawful confinement, and attempted murder written off."

"I concur."

Gilbert and Oscar had no sympathy for the twins. Then again, you couldn't expect them to easily forgive someone who almost killed their beloved. Oscar came up beside Gilbert.

"Eins is free to go, but I will have Zwei put on trial in accordance with the law."

"I will get the paperwork ready to file charges tomorrow. Until then, Zwei, you must remain—"

"No!"

The objection came from Cecilia. It was so unexpected that Oscar and Gilbert froze, confused. Tears in her eyes, Cecilia rose to her feet and pleaded to the duo in a shrill tone of voice.

"I'm sorry for worrying you! And for making you search for me all night! But I'm totally fine!"

"But the bruises—"

"Zwei and I were just fooling around! And the bruises are from when I tripped!"

"Those aren't the kind of bruises you can get from 'tripping'…"

Her version of events didn't hold water. She knew she wasn't convincing anyone. The bruises on her neck could have only been inflicted by someone strangling her, and the welts on her wrists had clearly resulted from them being bound with rope. Despite the fact she wasn't fooling anyone, Cecilia still had to say something, anything, to protect Zwei.

"If you so much as lay a finger on Zwei, I… I'll… I'll hate you both! A lot!"

Oscar's and Gilbert's attitudes changed at once. They didn't even need to exchange glances—her words had the same immediate effect on both of them.

"You'll…resent us?" Oscar repeated in a trembling voice.

"Come on now, Cecil, you're being overly emotional about this."

"No, I'm not! It's you two who are overreacting! I've been telling you Zwei didn't do anything bad!"

Cecilia rarely got riled up, hence why her fury was causing Oscar and Gilbert to lose confidence and exchange glances of consternation with each other. Nobody spoke for a while. Eventually, the silence was broken by Dante, who'd been quietly listening until then.

"He-he… He-he-he! Bwa-ha-ha-ha! Cecil, you're a piece of work!"

Dante roared with laughter, putting his hand over his stomach. Then he pushed past Oscar and Gilbert to stand next to Cecilia and placed his arm around her neck, as if to announce that he was siding with her.

"You'd better give up on that trial. Cecil's not going to agree to it."

"But consider the circumstances!"

"We can't just let Zwei off the hook…"

Dante ignored them and peered deep into Cecilia's eyes.

"So Cecil, what you're saying is you left the orphanage with Zwei to hang out elsewhere all night?"

"That's right!"

"And how did you get the bruises on your neck?"

"I tripped!"

"And the welts on your wrists?"

"I got caught in some vines!"

"Well, that explains everything."

Dante smiled, satisfied. Gilbert and Oscar exchanged looks again and sighed simultaneously, admitting defeat. Cecilia's defiant scowl was immediately replaced by a cheerful smile.

"So we're all good? That's great news, isn't it, Zwei?"

"Yes, but… Is this really okay with you?"

"Of course it is! We were just hanging out, after all," she repeated, giving Zwei's hand a squeeze.

"Thank you, Cecil. I'm really sorry for the trouble." He brightened up at last.

"Oh, but you'll have to apologize to Lean about the dress! She put a lot of work into making it, you know?"

"Of course, I'll do that! I don't know if it's within my capabilities, but I'll try to make a new dress to replace the one I ruined."

"There's no need for that," came a voice from the door.

Everyone turned. Lean entered the room, supported by Huey. Her feet were wrapped in bandages. Cecilia hurried over to her.

"Are you burned, Lean?!"

"They're very minor, thanks to your help. Doctor Mordred said they won't leave any scars…"

"So minor that she got bumped to the end of the line for treatment," snapped Huey, obviously annoyed. He'd probably had an argument with Mordred about it. Lean smiled at her boyfriend abashedly.

"Sorry, but why did you say I don't have to make a replacement costume?" Zwei asked, raising his hand as if he were in class.

Lean crossed her arms.

"Did you think I wouldn't have made a spare just in case? I made two of every costume to be on the safe side. So don't worry about crafting a replacement—I've already got it!"

"Wow, you're always well-prepared!" said Cecilia, impressed.

Lean smiled mischievously.

"You do owe me an apology, though, Zwei. And since you won't be making me a new costume, you'll have to make up for the trouble you caused in some other way."

"What should I do?"

Lean stood in front of him, leaning in so that their noses almost touched.

"You'll be helping me with the production, and boy, am I going to work you to the bone. Cecil's forgiven you, so I'm fine with keeping you on the team."

"Oh, um, all right! I'll do anything you say!"

"And the same goes for Eins."

"Okay."

Lean smiled with satisfaction when both of them agreed. Then she stepped away from the door, which suddenly swung open, as if someone had been waiting outside for the right moment. It was one of the waiters who worked at the academy lounge.

"I think we're all quite tired and could use a break, wouldn't you agree?" asked Lean.

"Um... I guess so?" Cecilia replied hesitantly.

"I put in an order for some food earlier. Why don't we all have dinner together? I haven't eaten anything since last night, and I'm starving!"

"There's venison, guys!" Jade poked his head through the door. He'd gone off to take a look at the festival, so he'd been absent from their informal gathering. Now he was back, pushing a trolley with plates of sautéed venison for everyone. "He-he! I got it for cheap from the same store we got the net from! The owner periodically goes deer hunting to get hides for making leather, so the meat's just a bonus for him. I talked him into selling it to me from now on. The price he's given me is thirty percent lower than the going wholesale price!"

"You sure have a nose for good deals," remarked Oscar.

"That's my one redeeming quality!" Jade joked, setting plates on the table.

Everyone found themselves a seat as the food Lean had ordered arrived.

"Whoa, will you look at that mountain of food?! It only just hit me how starving I am!" Jade was ready to chow down.

"I'm also starving. I need sleep, too, but food comes first," said Eins.

"It's my fault you've been up all night and didn't get to eat..."

"Don't worry about that, Zwei. You didn't do anything wrong. You were just hanging out with Cecil, isn't that right?" Dante reassured him.

"Is that the official version now?" Lean asked Huey who was next to her.

"Yes. If everyone's okay with it, I am, too."

"I've never dined like this. Do I pick a little from each platter?"

"That's right, Oscar! Isn't sharing food with everyone nice? Oh, by the way, do you want me to try the food before you eat it, in case it's poisoned?"

"He doesn't need you doing that for him, Cecil. Anyway, save your energy, you look dog-tired. What would you like to drink?"

Cecil, Oscar, and Gilbert chatted among themselves. Then there were two more recent arrivals standing in the doorway...

"I came here to look at Lean's burns, but perhaps now is not the time."

"It's a relief to see that everyone's in good spirits again."

Jade smiled at them affably and waved them in.

"Come and join us, Doctor!"

"Er..."

"And you too, Grace!" Cecilia chimed in.

"You want me to have dinner with you all?"

They were both rather reluctant. Jade and Cecilia stood up from their seats, walked over to them, and led them forcefully by their hands to a pair of empty seats.

"Now that's really everyone!"

"Perfect!"

Their mission accomplished, Jade and Cecilia returned to their seats. When each and every one of them was seated at the big table, Lean stood up and addressed them in her melodious voice.

"It was a challenging day, but thanks to all your hard work, it ended on a high note. Nice job, everyone!"

Cheers followed, and then they began their celebratory dinner.

About an hour in, Zwei finally stopped being so anxious. He was still looking a bit glum, but whenever someone chatted him up, he smiled and talked to them, and he readily answered questions without showing how fatigued he was. And if he didn't know what to say, Eins was there to take over. The twins were beginning to feel more at home.

Cecilia put a hand to her chest, relieved that they were gelling with the rest of her friends. She overheard their conversation with Jade, who was speaking quite loudly.

"So when you use Duplicate and Transfer together, it becomes Sharing?"

"That's right. You see, with Transfer, I lose something. With Duplication, Eins gains something. That's why when we use our abilities at the same time, they become Sharing."

"You guys have really useful skills! You could use Duplication to instantly replicate products to sell and then Transfer them to customers to save on shipping fees!"

Jade was talking to the twins more than anyone else. Not only was he a people person, but he also seemed genuinely interested in what they could do. Eins was quick to curb his enthusiasm, though.

"It's not that easy. Our abilities come with limitations and a high cost."

"What sort of limitations?"

"I need to understand an object's composition to successfully Duplicate it. That's why I can't Duplicate anything complex. Living creatures are also entirely impossible for me to copy."

"And I can only choose up to five destinations for Transfer."

"Okay, so Eins can only copy simple stuff, and you can only send things to a few set destinations?"

Zwei nodded.

"Yes, and I need to have touched a location beforehand to set it as a destination. I managed to send Cecil to Lean because I've touched her clothes, and I set that as one of the five destinations."

Cecilia was glad to finally understand how that worked. She'd freaked out a bit when Zwei had offered to teleport her to Lean. He hadn't explained it to her, either, so she had no clue where exactly she would land and how what he was doing was even possible.

Jade leaned closer to the twins.

"Tell me about the cost of your skills, then."

"It's hungry work. Using our abilities burns a lot of calories."

"While it depends on the size and complexity of objects for Eins and size and distance for me, Eins can generally use his powers up to twenty times a day. I can teleport up to three people a day before getting totally worn out."

"But your shared ability doesn't come with a price like that?"

"No, but we can't swap memories with anyone else."

So they could activate their abilities together to share memories without it taking a toll on either of them. You'd expect twins with special powers to have an ability they could only activate together. Jade seemed to think so as well.

"It's cool that you have a twins-only bonus ability."

"We always get a hankering for sugary drinks after using our personal skills."

"Or we go to the canteen and stuff ourselves with custard."

The twins looked at each other, smiling. Cecilia's head shot up as if something had suddenly occurred to her, and she rose from her chair.

"That reminds me!"

"Is something the matter, Cecil?"

"I got the recipe for that custard from the academy chef!"

Gilbert's face went blank with surprise. Cecilia smiled and walked over to the twins.

"So, you guys like custard? I can bake us one to share! Would you like that?"

"Sure, that'd be amazing. If it's not too much trouble, that is."

"You can really make it from scratch?"

"Yeah! Well, I say that, but I was actually thinking of preparing you a custard earlier, so I made one to test if it'd turn out okay. And it didn't..."

Cecilia scratched her cheek in embarrassment. One of the victims of her trial custard, Oscar, decided it was time to intervene.

"Didn't you agree not to try cooking anything at all until you figured out why your dessert was a disaster?"

"But I did! The chef explained to me where I went wrong!"

Cecilia smiled confidently, and Oscar went quiet. She puffed her chest out with pride.

"He said that beginners always misjudge the temperature! If you get the oven too hot, the custard starts, um, foaming? Bubbling? He said that he couldn't think of anything else that could've gone wrong."

"It's true that you got the temperature too hot. So hot that the top layer of the custard was indistinguishable from charcoal..." muttered Cecilia's second victim, Gilbert, while staring into the distance with a traumatized expression.

Gilbert had known from the start just how bad her cooking could be. Despite that, he would never refuse to eat anything she'd made—it was almost heroic of him.

As for the custard's third victim, he was shaking nervously, doing his best to avoid making eye contact with Cecilia. He'd rather not be asked to try her second attempt.

"So anyway, I was planning to make custards for everyone, and that includes you two, of course!"

"It sounds like a lot of work for you, though..."

"Not at all! And I promise to put in extra sugar to give you even more energy!"

That was a terrifying statement coming from someone who'd used a whole jar of sugar for her first attempt. Zwei had no idea that Cecilia had an unwitting knack for concocting poison out of the most unlikely ingredients, so he was only declining her offer out of politeness.

"I've caused you so much trouble already, and now you want to bake for me? It doesn't seem right."

"It'll be my pleasure to make something for you! I've been practicing especially for that!"

"But, still…"

"Lord Zwei." Lean put her hand on Zwei's shoulder. She smiled at him dazzlingly and said, "I think you ought to eat Cecil's custard."

"Um…"

"It will be the punishment you deserve."

Zwei froze up, confused at both her statement and the grin of wicked delight on her face.

"H-how is eating a custard a punishment?" he asked shakily.

"Lean, it's very rude of you to imply that eating Cecil's cooking is some kind of torture," Gilbert promptly scolded her.

Despite her friendly demeanor, Lean must have held quite the grudge against Zwei. She was about to urge him to take up Cecil's offer again when someone knocked on the door to the lounge.

"Come in!" said Oscar.

Two soldiers serving the Church walked in. They looked around and stood at attention.

"Our apologies for interrupting your dinner," they spoke briskly.

Everyone else in the room looked around uncertainly, wondering what this was about. The soldiers ignored the confusion their unannounced appearance caused.

"Holy Maiden Candidate Lean, the Holy Maiden wishes to see you and your knights. We ask you to please follow us to the shrine."

Cecilia had a sudden flashback to what Grace had told her earlier.

"In order to remove the Obstructions once and for all, you'll have to enter the shrine where the current Holy Maiden resides."

"Why is that?"

"There are several reasons, but the main one is that you need an item from there to exorcise away the Obstructions. Having the True

Love flag open is a requirement for entry. But once you get that item, there's no need to continue to that ending."

    Cecilia, Lean, and Grace exchanged glances, then nodded almost imperceptibly. There was no mistake.
    I've unlocked the True Love Route?!

"I'm sorry for telling Cecilia about your feelings. I jumped to the wrong conclusion, and I admit that even if I didn't, I should've kept my mouth shut. Anyway, could you give her this parcel?"

Lean, Gilbert's archnemesis, handed him a cloth-wrapped bundle about twenty minutes earlier.

"She's not exactly remorseful, is she…?"

It was the fourth day of the Week of Light. Gilbert and his friends had finally recovered from the trials and tribulations of Advent Day.

Gilbert headed over to Cecilia's apartment with the parcel—its contents a mystery to him—in one hand. The bundle was rectangular and felt soft. He peered inside through a gap in the wrapping and saw something made of fabric inside. Perhaps it was a costume or an outfit Lean had made for Cecilia.

"You can think of this parcel as compensation for my earlier indiscretion. Don't open it, though."

That's what Lean had told him when she gave him the parcel. What sort of compensation was this? He was just being used as a delivery boy.

Something tells me she's got an ulterior motive…

Yet he agreed to take the package to Cecilia himself, because it would make for a good excuse for him to check how she was doing. Not that he needed an excuse to go and see her, but it was more convenient this way.

Gilbert took a deep breath and knocked on Cecilia's door. He heard her calling "Coming!" in her usual cheery voice, and a moment later, the door opened.

"Oh, it's you, Gil! What's up?"

"Lean asked me to give this to you."

He held the parcel out to her, and she took it.

"It's good you turned up now, actually! Want to come in for some tea?"

"What's the occasion?"

"My fan club caught me at the festival and the girls gifted me a ton of cookies and snacks! Some of them don't keep long, and it's too much for me to eat by myself. So anyway, come on in!"

She took his hand and lead him inside. Gilbert hadn't been planning on staying, so he protested when she dragged him in, but she cheerfully ignored him.

Cecilia put the parcel from Lean on her bed and went to get some plates.

"I just got a teapot of black tea delivered from the kitchen."

"You know, actually, I think I'd rather go now..."

"If you hadn't shown up, I'd have invited Jade or Oscar or maybe Dante!"

Now that she'd said that, however, he was determined to sit it out.

"Really?" was all he managed to say, trying not to turn green with jealousy when his beloved casually told him she was going to invite some other guy to chill with her in her room. He sat down at the round table she had shown him to.

A few seconds later, he made a mental note to lecture her at another date.

Not only does she naturally lack a sense of danger, but she's been getting overly familiar with guys since she started dressing like a boy.

Cecilia was facing away from Gilbert, so she couldn't see the despondent look on his face. This was a prime example of her naïveté in social interactions—innocently inviting a boy she knew was in love with her to spend time alone with her in her apartment.

Or is it because she still just thinks of me as her brother?

"So what's in that parcel you brought me?" Cecilia's cheerful voice interrupted Gilbert's gloomy thoughts.

"You don't know, either?"

"Nope."

She set down cups of tea on the table and went to open the parcel.

"Oh wow, it's a yukata!" she exclaimed happily.

Gilbert turned to see it, having never heard of this article of clothing before.

"In my past life, we wore yukatas like this to festivals! Aw, the sash is so cute!" She was chirping happily, delighted at the gift. "I remember Lean saying the other day that she missed seeing people dressed in yukatas at festivals. And Advent is a festival, so I guess that's why she made this yukata for me!"

Cecilia lit up with excitement as she admired the yukata. Forgetting all about the tea and cookies, she leaned in toward Gilbert and looked at him pleadingly.

"Gil, do you mind if I try it on now?"

"I don't mind. Can you put it on without help?"

"Sure! I learned how to do the sash all by myself too!"

She picked up the yukata and disappeared in the adjacent room. For almost half an hour...

"Ta-daa!"

The person who emerged from the other room was not Cecil,

but unmistakably Cecilia. She wasn't wearing her short wig, and her outfit—a foreign garment the likes of which Gilbert had never seen before—revealed the curves of her body that she normally kept hidden. The garment sported a pattern of pink roses on a white background. The overlapping front of the robe was held closed by a burgundy sash wrapped below her breasts. Her hair was tied back in a simple way that went well with the outfit. The high overlapping collar was making the nape of her neck look very fetching.

"The pattern isn't in the Japanese style, so it might look a little strange."

"I wasn't expecting it to be a women's outfit."

"Yeah, it was a surprise! Isn't it pretty?"

It was pretty. She was pretty in it. No, gorgeous. The outfit disguised her childlike innocence and gave her a refined look that brought out her beauty. But there was one thing Gilbert didn't like about it.

"It doesn't offer you any protection."

While this "yukata" was undeniably a form of clothing, it was nothing more than a large piece of fabric with sleeves, secured with a belt. It reminded Gilbert of a bathrobe. If Cecilia tried to run wearing that, the sash would soon enough come undone and the whole thing would slip off.

"You think so?" Cecilia picked up the hem and turned around. "Well, it used to be worn to bed like pajamas in the past. I guess that's why it's so loose-fitting."

"It's a form of nightwear?"

"Yes, but it wasn't used like that anymore in my previous life." She paused, thinking. "Oh, except when staying at traditional Japanese inns."

Gilbert rubbed his forehead, trying to ease a sudden headache.

"So you do wear this to sleep. It's a nightdress."

"Yes... I mean, no. Let's not call it that, it would make things weird. It'd be almost as if I was showing you my negligee..."

Cecilia giggled and scratched her cheek, trying to cover up her embarrassment. Gilbert was about to ask her not to tease him by making him imagine her negligee when she said something that absolutely crushed him.

"Anyway, it's not like it matters, because it's only you, and maybe Lean, who will see me wearing it! Hmm, it would be okay to show it to Grace, too, I guess. Not Emily though. She's a girl but, you know, best to be on the safe side..."

That really stung. Gilbert hadn't felt this hurt in a while. "Only him" was already painful to hear, but being put in the same category as Grace and Lean made it worse. At the same time, Cecilia considered it inappropriate to wear that yukata in front of Emily, which placed Gilbert in a category completely outside any scope for potential romance. It wasn't because she thought of him as a brother or because she didn't see him as a man—it was because he was who he was that the possibility of this being a titillating situation never crossed her mind.

Gilbert wordlessly stood up and walked over to Cecilia.

"Do you want something?" she asked, but instead of replying, he pushed down on her shoulders and tripped her up with his foot.

"Wh-whoa!"

She fell over onto the bed, which was just behind her, her eyes open wide in shock. Gilbert interlaced his fingers with hers and leaned over the edge of the bed with his legs between hers, holding her down so that she couldn't get up. His voice became lower.

"I told you I love you, didn't I?"

"Um... Yeah, you did."

Cecilia looked up at him from the bed in confusion, her face bright red. She didn't seem to understand what he was getting at.

"Then maybe you could keep that in mind next time? It's really difficult for me to hold back, you know? Or maybe you don't want me to?" Gilbert whispered, their faces so close that he was tickling her with his bangs. Her cheeks turned a deeper shade of red, and her lips started to quiver. It delighted him to see his own reflection in her dilated pupils circled by sapphire-green irises. He squeezed her hands and touched his nose to hers.

"Well, if you're not saying anything..."

The next moment, something hit his head. It was only after he fell back onto his behind that he realized Cecilia had headbutted him. She had gotten up right in front of him with her legs wide apart, face all red, and traces of tears in her eyes. She was furious.

"Y-you perv! I don't want to see your face anymore! Get out!"

She pushed him out of her apartment, and he heard her locking the door behind him.

Did Cecilia just call me a perv?

Not that it wasn't justified. Still, she talked in such a childish way when she was angry.

Gilbert took one last look at her door and crouched down in the corridor.

"I went too far, I suppose. She may not want to talk to me for two, maybe three days."

Yet he felt in better spirits than before. The fact that he'd managed to make her blush and even get her to call him a perv meant that he wasn't just family to her anymore. He might have even turn her on a little.

I shouldn't feel so happy about her kicking me out.

A smile played on his lips. The small victory made his day.

"How was that yukata supposed to be Lean's compensation for me, though? Why should I care about a garment modeled on something from another world...? Oh, wait..."

It was only when he said it out loud that he made the connection. The reason Cecilia said she'd be okay showing the yukata to him, Lean, and Grace, but not Emily wasn't what he'd thought at first. And he could now see why Lean had made him deliver it as an apology to him.

"Damn..."

His earlier sense of victory vanished in an instant.

Yukatas didn't exist in this world. That's why Cecilia could only show off hers to other people who'd lived in her world before or who knew about her past life. Since Gilbert was one of them and he brought her the yukata, Lean had predicted that Cecilia would have the impulse to try on the outfit right away. And that was her gift to Gilbert—the sight of Cecilia in a yukata.

"I've been played..."

While it annoyed him that he'd unknowingly danced to someone else's tune, there was still a smile on his lips.

Advent period ended, and Vleugel Academy filled with students eager to learn new skills once again...

"Am I doing this right, Oscar?"

"That's not bad, but straighten your back more. Move your body in rhythm with the horse."

"Um, like this?"

Oscar and Cecilia were on the academy's riding grounds, with stables to one side and an indoor exercise facility on another. The two had changed into riding outfits, and Cecilia was sitting in front of Oscar on the back of a large horse as he taught her the basics of equestrianism. There wasn't much of a gap between them, and since Oscar had to reach around Cecilia to hold the reins with her, he was practically cuddling her.

"It's more difficult to keep steady than I thought."

"You'll get used to it. Don't turn to look at me, you're too close... Ahem, I meant to say, you may fall if you wriggle like that!"

"Sorry, sorry! So, face forward and match the horse's rhythm... Hmm... Ah... Ngh..."

"Please refrain from making noises like that!" Oscar exclaimed, blushing. He sighed and hung his head.

Why do I have to be tested so...?

He pursed his lips, trying to ignore the sweet scent of Cecilia's body, and thought back to the events that had led to this riding lesson.

It started with an unexpected announcement in the lecture hall the day before.

"Ahem... Boys will be starting horseback-riding lessons next week. I think most of you are familiar with the basics of equestrianism already, but don't think you can pass the course without making an effort. You will be learning dressage, show jumping, and eventing..."

The teacher, presumably their soon-to-be horseback-riding instructor, droned on as her bored pupils barely paid any attention. Except Cecilia, who was sitting next to Oscar. She had gone pale all of a sudden. Oscar felt her tugging at his sleeve. She was looking up at him, almost in tears.

"Oscar, what am I going to do? I've never ridden a horse..."

Of course she hasn't...

He half-closed his eyes in a fatigued expression. Girls would normally take up embroidery and party hosting courses in the last term of their second year at Vleugel, while boys would learn horse-riding instead. Girls could also learn equestrianism if they wanted, and likewise, no one would stop the boys from signing up for embroidery and hosting either, but the majority of students went with the default lesson program.

Oscar wouldn't expect a duke's daughter to have been taught horseback riding. Unlike girls of common background, aristocratic ladies simply didn't ride, unless they were, or aspired to become, knights.

Since Cecilia hadn't applied to switch to embroidery, Oscar had thought she might be able to ride, but now it was obvious that wasn't the case. She'd simply forgotten to put in the application to switch classes.

* * *

"I'm sorry to take up your time when you're so busy, Oscar…"

"Don't worry about it. And don't forget about body awareness."

"Ah, right. Straight back!"

She rubbed against him as she readjusted her position.

I've got to stop being so aware of HER body!

Oscar bit his lip, moving away from her as much as he could. That being said, it was practically impossible to avoid touching someone when you were riding a horse together. To make matters worse, a sweet scent like warm milk kept wafting from her every now and again.

"Are you wearing cologne?" Oscar eventually asked.

Cecilia replied without turning to look at him.

"No, why? Do I smell funny?"

"No…"

It's her natural smell?!

He felt as if he'd been struck by lightning. Cecilia was adorable, pretty, kind, and cheerful. And on top of all these loveable qualities, she even smelled sweet! It seemed almost unfair that she had so many amazing characteristics.

Another thing that took Oscar by surprise was how light and supple she felt. Whenever her back pressed against his chest or her upper arm against his, he marveled at how delicate it was, almost as if she was an entirely different kind of being from him. He yearned to hold her in a tight embrace—

Oscar slapped his cheek. The sound startled Cecilia and she turned to look at him.

"Wh-what was that? Why is your face so red?!"

"I killed a mosquito that landed on my cheek. Don't worry about it."

"How big was that mosquito for you to hit yourself in the face with so much force?"

"It was pretty big."

"Yikes. I'd better watch out," she said without a hint of sarcasm. Her naïveté was quite endearing.

Oscar cleared his throat and did his best to clear his mind, too, reminding himself to focus on the horseback-riding lesson.

"It was a shock to hear that everyone else already knew how to ride. You'd think the equestrianism classes would take you from the basics to the advanced stuff, but they assume you already have a foundation in it..."

"Most boys would have learned before attending the academy."

"But there must be other guys like me from families who don't ride."

Cecilia was getting used to being on horseback, chatting easily without having to concentrate on what she was doing.

"But at least this gave me a reason to learn. Since they call me the Prince of Vleugel Academy, I need to be able to handle a horse so that I can come to someone's rescue on a white steed one day."

"You complain about those girls following you around all the time, but you seem to want their attention," Oscar chuckled, nudging the horse to go faster.

Cecilia basked in the feeling of the wind in her hair.

"Woo-hoo! We're going so fast! This is great!"

"This is only a canter. Don't fall."

They did a lap and slowed down again. Cecilia turned toward Oscar, her eyes glinting with excitement.

"That was amazing! We rode so fast! I had no idea horseback riding was this fun!"

"It's even more fun once you learn to do it on your own."

"Really? I can't wait to get to that level!"

Her carefree smile warmed his heart. Cecilia's open and cheerful nature was perhaps what drew him to her the most. He loved her even more now than when he'd fallen for her at first sight twelve

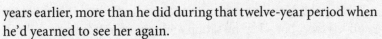

years earlier, more than he did during that twelve-year period when he'd yearned to see her again.

"Also, horses are really tall! It's refreshing to see everything from a different perspective."

"I'm used to that, I suppose."

"Ah, so this is how you normally view the world. Wow!"

She faced forward again as if to take it all in.

"It's nice that I get to share this experience with you!"

Those words were more poignant to him than she had intended. He'd been dreaming about this for a while, after all. Oscar had wanted to share his life with her ever since their engagement had been formalized.

"I'd like to see many more things together with you."

He was thinking about their future together, as a royal couple, when he said that. Of course, Cecilia had no inkling that he meant it that way. She smiled at him.

"Sure, let's see all sorts of places together! Anything's fun when you're around!" she paused for a moment. "Will you teach me how to hunt next time?"

Oscar smiled awkwardly and stopped the horse. Then he dismounted, leaving Cecilia on her own atop the horse.

"Let's take a break. After that, you'll do a lap on your own."

"Sounds good! Let's do tha—" Cecilia's leg slipped out of the stirrup when she was getting off the horse and she lost her balance. "Whoa, whoa!"

Oscar extended his hand on reflex. He caught Cecilia by the wrist as she was about to fall down head first, extended his free arm to support her back, and swiftly moved to stand directly underneath her.

Bam! Oscar found himself spread-eagled on the ground, with Cecilia on top of him. Something soft was pressed against his cheek.

What is this doughy softness?

He grabbed the mysterious squishy object with his hand to get it off his face, but when he sat up and saw what it was, he froze. It was Cecilia's breast. She'd tightly bound her chest under her clothes to make it appear flat, but what he was feeling in his hand was still undoubtedly a breast. Cecilia, still straddling him, blushed a little. She pointed to his hand.

"Oscar, um, do you mind removing your hand?"

He didn't make a sound, but inwardly, he was screaming.

Afterword

Hello, dear readers. I'm Hiroro Akizakura.

After a year-long wait, the third volume of *Cross-Dressing Villainess Cecilia Sylvie* is finally here. Ideally, if I do write another volume, I'd like to get it published sooner rather than later, but no matter how hard I try, I just can't manage to output one novel every two or three months, so please be patient! I finished this one off in a way that begs for continuation, so I promise that I'll prioritize finding time to write more!

But whether what I write gets published or not depends on the sales of the already released volumes, so you could say the future of the series is in your hands! Please help me out and buy my books! *humble bow*

Okay, that bowing and prostrating myself on the ground was a good warm-up exercise. Time to get back to the main topic: my remarks for this volume! I've got three pages allocated for the afterword this time, so I don't have to be so economical with words!

Let me tell you first about the cover! Dangmill provided a wonderful cover illustration yet again. Isn't Oscar and Gilbert's stare-off just delightful? I can't help grinning every time I look at it! And the way they're holding the flowers really reflects their personality, I think! I love it! (Aah, sudden confession!)

Now, as for the story, I think I went a bit overboard this time. By writing too much, I mean. This volume ended up over the length my Japanese publisher usually prints, but thanks to my wonderful editor, it got approved. Thank you so much, dear editor, and sorry for the extra trouble.

I've been having so much fun serializing the story online that I simply couldn't stop writing. This time, I've been channeling my efforts into romance scenes with Oscar and Gilbert, and once I got into it, I wanted to keep churning out the pages.

I had so much fun creating this story for you. I hope you'll enjoy reading it just as much!

I've been getting more readers who first found out about the series by reading the manga version by Shino Akiyama lately. I'm so grateful to her for her incredible work! Her drawings add so much life to the characters. I think her manga is even better than my novels! So check it out if you haven't already done so! Shino's manga made me fall in love with the *Cross-Dressing Villainess* character cast even more!

This volume also comes with an extra special bonus: a voiced recording of Gilbert and Oscar! Yay! Applause!

Buy the book to get the audio drama as a bonus! I wrote the scenario for it, of course! It's only available for a limited time, so make sure not to miss out on your chance to hear the sensual voices of Gilbert and Oscar.

Besides the audio drama, I also wrote some other short pieces for you to enjoy.

I never thought I'd be able to offer such cool bonuses with my book. I've got all of you to thank for making it possible!

Thank you so much to Dangmill, Shino Akiyama, my editor, and everyone at the publisher's office who helped with the book, including the proofreader, admin, design, and printing staff, and also all the bookstores that stock my novels.

But most of all, thank you to all my readers!

I'm so grateful to have you! I really am super lucky!

I'm going to do my best writing the continuation of the story for you. It'd be amazing if you keep cheering me on! Fingers crossed we meet again in the next volume!

Hiroro Akizakura

HAVE YOU BEEN TURNED ON TO LIGHT NOVELS YET?

86—EIGHTY-SIX, VOL. 1-11

In truth, there is no such thing as a bloodless war. Beyond the fortified walls protecting the eighty-five Republic Sectors lies the "nonexistent" Eighty-Sixth Sector. The young men and women of this forsaken land are branded the Eighty-Six and, stripped of their humanity, pilot "unmanned" weapons into battle...

Manga adaptation available now!

WOLF & PARCHMENT, VOL. 1-6

The young man Col dreams of one day joining the holy clergy and departs on a journey from the bathhouse, Spice and Wolf. Winfiel Kingdom's prince has invited him to help correct the sins of the Church. But as his travels begin, Col discovers in his luggage a young girl with a wolf's ears and tail named Myuri who stowed away for the ride!

Manga adaptation available now!

SOLO LEVELING, VOL. 1-5

E-rank hunter Jinwoo Sung has no money, no talent, and no prospects to speak of—and apparently, no luck, either! When he enters a hidden double dungeon one fateful day, he's abandoned by his party and left to die at the hands of some of the most horrific monsters he's ever encountered.

Comic adaptation available now!

THE SAGA OF TANYA THE EVIL, VOL. 1–10

Reborn as a destitute orphaned girl with nothing to her name but memories of a previous life, Tanya will do whatever it takes to survive, even if it means living life behind the barrel of a gun!

Manga adaptation available now!

SO I'M A SPIDER, SO WHAT?, VOL. 1–15

I used to be a normal high school girl, but in the blink of an eye, I woke up in a place I've never seen before and—and I was reborn as a spider?!

Manga adaptation available now!

OVERLORD, VOL. 1–14

When Momonga logs in one last time just to be there when the servers go dark, something happens—and suddenly, fantasy is reality. A rogues' gallery of fanatically devoted NPCs is ready to obey his every order, but the world Momonga now inhabits is not the one he remembers.

Manga adaptation available now!

VISIT YENPRESS.COM TO CHECK OUT ALL OUR TITLES AND. . .

GET YOUR YEN ON!